Meg Perry

Burdened to Death

A Jamie Brodie Mystery

The Jamie Brodie Mysteries:

Cited to Death

Hoarded to Death

Burdened to Death

Sunday, March 17, 2013

A phone call in the middle of the night is never good news.

Technically, it wasn't the middle of the night. It was 5:00 am. But it was Sunday. My boyfriend Pete and I had hiked all day Saturday in Topanga Canyon with my brother Kevin and his girlfriend Abby. We'd covered a lot of territory and we'd been bushed when we got home. So the plan had been to sleep in this morning.

So much for that.

It was Pete's phone. He disentangled himself from me and the sheets and snagged it off the bedside table. "H'lo." I could only hear his side of the conversation.

"Kev. What the hell. *What?*" He sat up quickly, pulling the comforter off of me. I grunted and tugged at it.

"What's the guy's name?" Pete gasped. "Yeah, I know him. He was a friend of ours in Barstow." *Barstow*. Pete's hometown until he was fourteen. A place of excruciating memories.

"Um – yeah, I could do that. When? Oh. Yeah, okay. Where are you?"

Whatever Kevin said made Pete turn and look at me. "Okay. We'll be there in a bit." He said goodbye and hung up, then just sat there, phone dangling from his hand, staring at the opposite wall.

I managed to roll over and switched on the bedside lamp. "What?"

"Kevin got called out on a body and he needs me to identify it."

"Why you?"

"The guy had one of my cards in his pocket. His name is Mark Jones."

"Mmph. Where are we going?"

"Kevin said the building is where your old boyfriend Eric lives."

"Ah." Eric was an LA County paramedic that I'd dated nearly three years ago. He lived in an apartment complex in Westwood. "It's on Midvale."

"Okay." Pete gave the comforter a final shove to the foot of the bed. "Have to get dressed and get over there."

At 5:30 a.m. on Sunday there was very little traffic between our townhouse in Santa Monica and the apartment complex. Once we were underway I asked, "So you knew this guy in Barstow?"

"Yeah. He was a year ahead of me in school, right between Steve and me. He lived down the street. He was the only person I stayed in touch with after we moved to my dad's. Then we went to UCLA at the same time."

"How'd he get one of your cards?"

"I ran into him about a year ago at Trader Joe's. Hadn't seen him for years. He said he'd like to catch up, and I gave him one of my cards, wrote my cell number on the back. But I never heard from him, and I kind of forgot about it."

Uh oh. Pete was a psychologist. A friend who'd committed suicide was going to stir up significant guilt. I laid my hand on his thigh. "Did you have his number?"

"No."

"Then it was up to him to call if he wanted to talk to you. You had no way of knowing."

"I could have looked for him."

"Did he seem suicidal a year ago?"

"No. He seemed fine."

"Then don't beat yourself up over this."

"I won't."

But I knew better.

We zipped up Wilshire and parked in front of the building. The street wasn't blocked, but there were two patrol cars and a fire truck. My brother Kevin was an LAPD homicide detective. He and Abby lived just a few hundred yards from here, in an apartment on

Roebling. He'd arrived at the scene on foot and met us at the front of the building. "Hey. Sorry to drag you out like this."

I said, "Where's Tim?" Tim Garcia was Kevin's partner.

"Since it was a probable suicide, I said I'd handle it. He didn't need to come all this way."

Pete asked, "You're sure about the suicide?"

"Yeah. The coroner will have the final word, but there's not much doubt. He hung himself from his own balcony. I just need to be sure it's him before I notify the family."

Pete looked grim. "Where is he?"

Kevin said to me, "Stay put." He led Pete into the courtyard of the building. I waited. The firefighters came out, loaded up their equipment and left.

Kevin and Pete returned shortly thereafter. Pete said, "It was him."

We tried to avoid displays of affection in public, but I put my arm around his shoulders and gave him a quick half-hug. Kevin said, "I've got work to do. Talk to you all later." He went back into the courtyard.

Pete turned to me. "Want to go to Headlines?"

"It's only 6:00. I doubt they're open."

"Oh. Any ideas?"

We ended up at Izzy's Deli, not one of our usual haunts, but open 24 hours and close to home. We parked at the house and walked to the deli. Pete was quiet. I didn't ask any questions – I figured he needed time to process.

We both ordered pancakes. I finally asked, tentatively, "Was it bad?"

"Not the worst I've seen." Before earning his Ph.D., Pete was a cop. He and Kevin were partners during Kevin's first five years as an LAPD patrol officer and had been close friends ever since.

I knew Pete had seen bad stuff as a cop, but it had to be different when it was someone you knew. I said, "At least it wasn't a gunshot."

"Yeah. That would have been worse." Pete rubbed his face again. "I don't think he'd been there long."

"Had you always known him?"

"Pretty much. He moved to our street when I was six. His dad was at Edwards. They'd been living on base but finally bought a house."

"He must have been a good friend if you stayed in touch after you left Barstow."

"He was." Pete didn't say any more. He seemed lost in thought.

I didn't push it. I knew Barstow brought back a lot of awful memories for Pete. His parents had divorced when he was ten, and as a fourteen-year-old altar boy, he'd been sexually abused by a priest. When Pete's dad had found out, he'd moved Pete and his older brother Steve to live with him in Lancaster. Pete had begun counseling almost immediately and had come a long way. But he still had issues because of the abuse.

Our pancakes came and we ate, talking about other things. When we finished we decided to go to Vons and get our groceries for the week. Pete was still preoccupied, though. When we got home I said, "Let's get in the shower."

In the shower, I worked on loosening the knots in Pete's shoulders. Then I worked on another part of his anatomy. By the time we finished we were both clean and relaxed. We put on sweats and settled on the living room sofa with the newspaper. I was reading the comics when Pete laid down his section. "I don't know why Mark would do this."

"You really didn't know much about his adult life, right?"

"Right. When I saw him a year ago we didn't talk much. Just the standard 'what are you doing now' stuff. He told me he had a boyfriend, and I told him I did too. That's when he said he'd like to get together, and I gave him my card. And that was it."

"A year ago? We hadn't started dating yet."

He gave me a sly smile. "No. But I knew we were going to."

I laughed. "Pretty confident, were you?"

"Yep."

"Did you know he was gay?"

"No."

"Pretty brave to come out to you like that, after not seeing you for so many years."

"It was. He was like that. Always positive, always determined. It's hard to imagine the kid I knew committing suicide."

"People change."

"I know."

"Is Kevin sure it was suicide?"

"Yeah. The way it happened – there'd be no way someone could stage that."

"Kevin referred to a roommate – do you think that's his boyfriend?"

"I guess so."

"Was Kevin going to notify the right people?"

"The roommate was listed as first emergency contact. Kevin was going to call him first, to get the family's phone numbers. If it was his boyfriend, then at least Kev was notifying him first."

"Good. You know – if you wanted to know more about why he did this, I could look into it."

"How? It's a suicide. There's no case."

"You're thinking like a cop. The police don't have a case, true, but I could at least find out as much as I could about him. Maybe it would give you some – I hate this word, but I'll use it for lack of a better one – closure."

"How would you go about this?"

"Newspaper archives. We have every issue of the LA Times. And I'll Google him and see what comes up. Once I learn more about him, I can research the company he worked for, organizations he was involved in. I can get into government records." I poked him in the ribs. "I'm a librarian. Never underestimate my ability to find shit out."

He laughed. "Yeah, but the first time you went on a quest to find shit out, someone tried to kill us. And the second time, someone tried to kill Jennifer."

Jennifer was Kevin's ex-wife.

"Details, details. Anyway, this time I'm not trying to uncover a killer. I'm just trying to get you some answers about your friend."

Pete leaned over and kissed me. "You're a good boyfriend."

"Thank you. I try."

It was nice to banter with Pete. We hadn't been doing much of that lately. We'd started dating – for the second time – about nine months ago. Less than a week later an arsonist had burned me out of the apartment I'd been sharing with Kevin and Abby. I'd moved in with Pete on what was supposed to be a temporary basis, and I never left. We'd been doing great until last Christmas when Pete told me about his abuse.

Pete's admission had impacted our sex life. I'd been frustrated at the lack of variety in our bedroom – Pete would only top, and I liked to take turns. I'd been ready to suggest that to him when he dropped the bombshell. I certainly understood why he'd only top. But Pete's news didn't help alleviate the physical frustration I felt – it made it worse, since it seemed that things were not likely to change. A couple of months ago I'd begun seeing a counselor, in hopes of learning to deal with the frustration without taking it out on Pete. It was definitely helping. Dr. Bibbins had made several behavioral suggestions that would help me deal with my emotions.

But things were slightly strained between us. Pete had been upset by the news that I was seeing a counselor. He felt guilty, and he was afraid that I'd eventually leave him. Ironic, since he was the one who left me when we'd dated before.

Doctoral candidates in psychology are required to undergo psychotherapy as part of their training. Pete was still with the therapist that he'd begun seeing in his Ph.D. program. It had been six years now. I hadn't seen any indication that this therapist was helping him. His behavior and emotions hadn't changed much since – well, since I'd known him, which was also six years. He said that he wanted to work on our relationship – but so far I seemed to be the only one doing any work.

Monday, March 18

The next morning, at breakfast, I opened the Evernote app on my iPad. "I need to get more detail about your friend. Mark Jones, right?"

"Right."

"Do you know his middle name?"

"Um – David."

"Date of birth?"

"His birthday was April 22nd. And he was a year ahead of me in school, so probably 1974."

"What high school did he go to?"

"There's only one. Barstow High School."

"No private schools?"

"No."

"Do you remember his parents' names?"

"No. I could ask my dad, he'd probably remember."

"I've got his address from the apartment building – do you know what kind of work he did?"

"He didn't say where he worked, but he was an actuary."

"Oh. Interesting. And he was at UCLA with you?"

"Yeah. He took a year off between high school and college, so he was in the same graduating class as me. We had an economics class together freshman year, or I'd probably never have seen him."

"Wonder why he took a year off?"

Pete shook his head. "No idea." He nodded at my iPad. "Think you've got enough to get started with?"

"Absolutely." I closed the iPad's cover and looked at my watch. "I'd better go." I leaned over the table to kiss him. "See you tonight."

This week was the last of the winter quarter at UCLA. It wasn't an especially busy time for us librarians. Most students had finished their research and were now writing their papers or studying for exams. I was teaching a course, Historical Research Methods, in the spring quarter, and I needed to get it set up this week. But other than that, I didn't have anything pressing. I should have some time to find out about Pete's friend.

I spent the morning working on my class – updating the syllabus and schedule, and rewriting the assignments. I'd originally intended to teach history, so this course filled that desire in me for classroom instruction. I changed the assignments and project requirements every year to discourage blatant plagiarism. Most of the students in the MLIS program were upstanding citizens, but you never knew when you'd get a lazy one.

At 1:00, I met Liz Nguyen at the reference desk for our two-hour shift. Liz was my best friend at work, a gorgeous Hawaiian/French/Vietnamese-American who had been a year behind me in library school. She was dating another friend of mine, a homicide detective with LAPD's Pacific Division named Jon Eckhoff. I'd introduced Jon and Liz back in December, and they'd been inseparable ever since. They joined Pete and me, when they could, on our weekend hiking expeditions.

Every day at 1:30, Liz and I were visited by Clinton Kenneally, a retired Benedictine monk, who gave us a word of the day. Clinton had a knack for choosing words that had something to do with what was going on in our lives. Today, when he approached the desk, Liz said, "Hi, Clinton."

He smiled at us. "The word of the day is *benedict*." He bowed at the waist and turned to go.

Liz got out the notebook in which we kept Clinton's words. "Doesn't that mean - something good? *Bene* means well in Latin."

"Yeah, like a benediction at the end of a church service. But it's also the name of the ex-pope. And the patron saint of Clinton's order." I looked up the word online and was surprised. "Huh. It means 'a newly married man who has long been a bachelor.'"

Liz tapped my shoulder with her pencil. "He's talking about you."

"*Me?* I'm not newly married."

"No, but you're newly partnered. You're living with a guy for the first time since Ethan, long term. Right?"

"I am living with a guy for the first time since Ethan. I *hope* it's long term."

Liz frowned. "What do you mean, you *hope?* You're not giving up already?"

"Of course not."

She lowered her voice and scooted over so that she could nearly whisper. "I *told* you not to fuck this up."

"I'm *not*." I really didn't want to get into the gory details with Liz, but… "This time it's not me, okay? It turns out that Pete and I are not – um – completely compatible in one very important area. *I'm* working on it. He's not."

"*Oh*." Liz scooted back to her side of the desk. "That's a surprise."

"Jeez. Thank you very much."

She smacked me lightly on the arm. "Not that *you're* working on it, doofus. That he's *not*. That surprises me."

"I'm not thrilled by it either."

"So what are you going to do about it?"

"I'm working with a counselor to learn how to manage it from my end. For now, that's all I can do. I'm not going to give Pete ultimatums. Ultimata?"

"Either one." Liz gave me a sympathetic smile. "I'm sorry you guys are having problems."

"Me too. I'm sure we'll work it out somehow." But I wasn't, really.

At 3:00, Liz and I went back to our offices. I spent the next couple of hours doing some preliminary investigating into Pete's friend. When I Googled "Mark David Jones" with "Los Angeles" I got a couple of obituaries (not the one for Pete's friend – it was too soon for that), a couple of LinkedIn profiles, an Ancestry.com link, a person of the same name from Texas, and a bunch of Facebook profiles that I couldn't see without logging in. I hadn't joined Facebook and didn't want to do so just to see if Mark Jones was there. From the little information I could glean, there were a bunch of guys named Mark Jones in LA, which you'd expect for such a common name. I also discovered that I really hated Facebook's search function.

Next I tried "Mark David Jones" with "actuary." There was one gent with that name and occupation in the UK, but not in LA. Taking out the "David" resulted in more hits, but mostly relating to the UK's Mark Jones. When I added "Los Angeles" to "Mark David Jones" and "actuary," I got nothing.

It's not often that you can stump Google.

At 5:00, I gave up and went home. When I got there, Pete had dinner ready. That was almost always the case. He was a terrific partner in so many ways. He was attentive, romantic, thoughtful, generous, smart, and funny. We had similar tastes in so many things. We never ran out of things to talk about. He was flat-out gorgeous. He loved my family. Hell, he loved *me*.

But when it got down to the nitty-gritty of fucking…not so much.

Dinner was delicious. We talked about our days as we ate paella. Pete was up for tenure at Santa Monica College and was expecting to hear the decision soon. We talked about a guy in another department that probably wasn't going to get tenure, and I reassured Pete that he had nothing to worry about. Then I told him about my Google search for Mark Jones.

"There was nothing at all?"

"Not yet. I haven't tried searching with his address or birthdate, though. Apparently he hasn't done anything outstanding in his profession. I was on lots of actuarial organization websites this afternoon, and his name didn't turn up."

"I'm not entirely surprised. He was always one to fly under the radar as much as he could."

"Was he shy?"

"He was definitely an introvert, but it wasn't that. His parents got divorced a couple of years after mine. My parents seethed in silence, but his had knock-down, drag-out fights. We could hear them from our front porch sometimes. I think he got used to melting into the woodwork."

"Was he an only child?"

"No, he had an older sister. She was about the same age as my sister but they weren't friends."

"What was her name?"

"Um – Marcia. Like Marcia Brady. I remember because we'd tease her – 'Marcia, Marcia, Marcia.'"

I laughed. "You were obnoxious little brothers."

He grinned. "Yeah, like you weren't."

"Oh, I was, trust me. Just ask Kevin or Jeff."

Pete's smile faded. "I'd like to go to his memorial service."

"I'll keep checking the Times website. His obituary and arrangements should be there soon."

"Will you come with me?"

"Sure, if you want me to."

"I do."

I'd cleared the dinner dishes and we were eating dessert – key lime pie – when I suddenly remembered that I had a counseling session tomorrow and I hadn't done my homework. "I forgot to tell you what my assignment was from Dr. Bibbins for this week."

"What was it?"

"I told her that you hadn't said what you were doing in therapy for about a month, and she said I should ask you this week. So, what have you been doing in therapy lately?"

He gave me a measured look. "Funny you should ask this week. Last Thursday, we talked for a while about you."

"How so?"

"The therapist was getting into our different coping styles. I told her that you were more upset than I expected when I told you about my abuse. She suggested that was because you'd been more coddled in your life up to now than I have been."

What the *fuck??* And we'd been having such a nice evening. I laid down my fork very carefully, so I wouldn't be tempted to stab him with it, and pushed back from the table a little. "*Excuse* me? *Coddled? Are you serious?*"

Pete kept eating, calmly. "I told her I didn't think that was the best choice of words."

"And what word did *you* suggest?"

Pete seemed to finally sense that there might be some danger here. He laid down *his* fork. "I said that sheltered might be a better word."

"*Sheltered.* And what *the fuck* do you base that on?"

"Now, don't get bent out of shape, just think about it. And remember this is in comparison to me. You grew up in a stable, loving home. I'm the product of a broken home. You never were abused in any way; obviously I was. You've never faced any kind of discrimination or problems because you were gay; you've spent your entire adult life in relatively safe academia. I put up with a *lot* of that when I was on the police force. And… You've never had anything bad happen to you. I saw stuff when I was a cop that you can't even *imagine.*"

Hoo boy. I stood up, gripped the back of the chair, and leaned over the table. "Well, Dr. Ferguson, since I'm so steeped in academia, let me *educate* you a little bit. First, about that stable, loving, unbroken home. My home broke, I just wasn't old enough to remember it. I grew up watching my dad grieve *every day* for my mom. Every time one of us hit a milestone of any sort, it *killed* him that she wasn't there to see it. Until I was five or six years old, I remember him crying *every night* when he tucked us into bed. It took *years* for the overlay of sorrow to lift, for my dad to become the cheerful guy you know today."

Pete had a guarded look on his face. "I didn't know that."

"No, you didn't. And here's something else you don't know. You think I've never had any problems because I was gay? My grandfather has not spoken to me since the *moment* he found out I was gay. The man who helped raise me, who spent hours hitting me grounders and helped me study for exams and brought me 7-Up with crushed ice when I was sick, has not spoken *one word* to me, has not even acknowledged my *existence* since I was fifteen."

Now Pete looked stricken. "I thought your grandfather was dead."

"Oh, no. The old bastard's alive and well in an assisted living facility in Jacksonville, North Carolina, near my Uncle Doug's house. He sends birthday cards to Jeff and Kevin, and even to Jeff's kids. He calls my dad every week and doesn't even ask if I'm still *alive*. If my dad mentions my name, even in passing, my grandfather *hangs up* on him. When Kevin graduated from high school, my grandfather moved out of our house the *next day*. He couldn't get away from me fast enough. How's *that* for a problem?"

"That's… I'm sorry. That's bad."

"You bet your ass that's bad." I'd let go of the chair and was pacing now. "And here's something else. You didn't get drafted into the police academy, you *chose* to be a cop. You could have just as easily gone directly into academia yourself, or you could have left the force even sooner than you did. You *chose* that, for whatever reason. So don't hold that up as something equivalent to the abuse, as something that happened to you and you couldn't avoid."

I could tell Pete was cringing inwardly. "Okay. That's fair."

"*Damn* straight." I was on a roll now. "And one more thing. Here's something I know for a *fact*. You've *never* had your heart broken. You've never stood in a cold room and listened to the love of your life tell you that he's leaving, and watch all the plans you had for the future crumble into dust at your feet. You've never had to completely reinvent yourself because half of your life, your *better* half, just walked out the door. So don't tell *me* I've never had anything bad happen to me. No, it's nowhere near as bad as the abuse. But just like I can't imagine what you went through with that, *you* don't know what *I* went through when Ethan left. Because that's never happened to you. You've ended exactly two relationships, one of them with *me*, and each time it's been *your* choice. So don't tell me how I should react to *anything*. Because you don't *know*." I was out of breath, and could tell that I was starting to not make sense. So I stopped and just glared at Pete.

To his credit, he was pale and chagrined. "You're right. I guess I…" He stopped, then shook his head. "You're right."

"And you can tell your fucking *therapist* that she needs to say shit like that to my *face*."

"She was just basing that on what I'd told her about you."

"Well, then, you'd better set her straight."

"I will."

"You'd *better*."

"I *will*."

"*Fine*." I was completely out of juice now. I pulled my chair back out and sat down, arms crossed.

Pete had picked his fork up and was rearranging the crumbs on his plate into abstract patterns. "So…Ethan was the love of your life."

Oh, jeez. Suddenly I was very tired. "I thought so, at the time."

"And you didn't see the breakup coming?"

"No. We'd been having some problems, but we'd been together seven years. I thought we were just going through a slump."

"Seven years. That's a long time."

"Yep."

"You loved him."

I sighed. "Yeah, I did. Don't try to compare, Pete. I was a lot younger then. It was different than now."

"And you haven't seen or heard from him since."

"No."

"Do you know where he is?"

"When he left Oxford, he was moving to Connecticut to get his Ph.D. at Yale. I don't know where he went from there."

And that was the end of it.

Tuesday, March 19

Dr. Bibbins tapped her pen on the page of the notebook. "Was that the end of it?"

"Yeah. I got up and cleared the table, we washed dishes and went to bed. We haven't talked about it anymore." I opened my lunch. Dr. Bibbins poured me a cup of Earl Grey and set it on a coaster on the end table at my side.

"What do you have for lunch today?"

"Hummus and veggies on pita." I showed her. "And a cookie."

"Is that homemade hummus?"

"Yeah. The cookie too. Pete baked on Sunday."

"Do you ever cook?"

"Sometimes. I make chili and spaghetti sauce, big-batch stuff like that. I like to use the crock pot." I took a sip of tea. "My grandfather taught me to cook."

"When you were younger."

"Yeah. Before he stopped talking to me."

"Yes. That must have been painful for you."

"It was. But it also showed me what could happen with coming out, that not everyone would react well, even if it was someone that supposedly loved you. So it made me a lot more cautious than I might have been otherwise. Silver linings, right?"

"Right." She took a sip of tea, then set her cup down. "Let me ask you this. Have you seen any significant change in Pete's behavior or emotion since January?"

"He's quieter. Other than that, no. I don't think his therapist is doing much to help our situation."

"Why do you say that?"

"He's been seeing her since his Ph.D. program."

"And how long has that been?"

"Six years. I know he's come a long way in terms of his own thoughts and emotions, but I think that work was done by the therapist he saw when he was a teenager. And I definitely don't think his psychotherapy is doing anything for *us*. For our relationship."

"No. It's not going to. Psychotherapy is about the individual. The relational problems that you're experiencing would be more successfully addressed by cognitive behavioral therapy, which can be done in a couples setting."

"I think at this point his therapist is just enabling him. And I think she's painting me as the bad guy."

"The therapist he has now is allowing him to remain in a comfortable place."

"Yes. And he's agreeing with her that I've been *sheltered*. God knows what else she's got him thinking about me."

"Are you telling Pete what we discuss?"

"Yeah. I haven't kept anything hidden from him."

"Good. It concerns him and your relationship, so he has a right to know. Just as you have a right to know what his therapist is telling him about you and your relationship. You got a bit sidetracked last night, but you need to ask him if he and the therapist are working on your relationship issues."

"Okay. I will."

"We've covered a lot of ground since January. How are you feeling about your progress?"

I considered. "I feel good. I'm not feeling as - panicked, I guess? And I think I can cope better with the frustration now."

"I'm glad to hear that. I believe we've come as far as we can without Pete's participation. Do you think there's a chance he would consider couples therapy?"

"Oh boy. I doubt it. At least not at this point."

"All right. What we'll do next week is review the coping strategies we've covered and the insights you've gained. Then, unless you object, I think you're ready for discharge. Of course you can come back at any time."

I nodded. "That sounds reasonable."

"Good. I'll see you next week."

After my session with Dr. Bibbins, it was time for my reference shift. Clinton's word of the day was *hawkshaw*. Liz looked it up. "You're not going to believe this."

"What?"

"It means *detective*." She frowned at me. "You're not getting involved in another police case, are you?"

"Well – not exactly."

"Oh my God. I knew it. What does *not exactly* mean?"

"It means it's not a police case. But I am looking into something. A childhood friend of Pete's committed suicide Saturday night. It upset him a little, as you'd expect. So I told him I'd try to find out a little about the guy's life, to see if there were any answers to the question of why he did it."

"And it's definitely a suicide."

"That's what Kevin said."

"Kevin was there?"

"The guy lived here in Westwood, near where I used to live. Kevin was up for a case, and they called him to take a look, but he said he was as sure as he could be before autopsy that it was a suicide."

"Did the guy leave a note?"

I stared at Liz for a second. "I'm an idiot. Because I never thought to ask. *Duh.*"

Liz laughed. "When we get done here, call Kevin and find out."

So I did. I figured I'd have to leave a voicemail, but Kevin answered immediately. "Hey."

"You're not busy?"

"I need a break from paperwork, so I answered the phone. What's up?"

"I have a weird request. About Pete's friend who killed himself."

"What about him?"

"Well, first, are you sure it's a suicide?"

"The autopsy hasn't been done yet, so it's not official. But yeah, I'm sure."

"Did he leave a note?"

"Not that we could find. Not everyone does."

"No, I guess not."

"Why do you want to know?"

"Pete was kind of – not really upset, more like just baffled as to why Mark would kill himself. So I told him I'd look into his life, see if I could uncover anything."

"And have you?"

"No. But I've just started looking. I did a Google search yesterday and found nothing. So far the guy has no online footprint."

"Hm. If you do find anything, let me know. The boyfriend is looking for answers, too."

"So the roommate was his boyfriend."

"Yeah. They'd been together about a year and a half."

"And the boyfriend didn't have any idea why he might have done it?"

"No. But the guy was too upset to think. He said he'd call if he remembered anything."

"When is his autopsy going to be done?"

"Tomorrow. Toxicology will take longer, but the ME should be able to give us a pretty good idea."

"Will they release his body after that? Pete wants to go to his funeral."

"Yeah, they'll have it by tomorrow evening, unless something weird turns up."

"Would you mind letting me know? When you find out?"

"What, that the body's been released, or that it was really suicide?"

"Both."

"Sure, I'll add you to the list."

"There's a list?"

"Boyfriend, mother, father, sister. Apparently most of the relatives don't speak to each other."

"Oh jeez."

"No kidding." Kevin's voice softened a fraction. "Isn't Tuesday counseling day for you? How's that going?"

"It's going fine from my end. Pete told me last night that his therapist believes I've been coddled in my life."

"What the *fuck?*"

"My sentiments exactly. I kind of yelled at him about it. For several minutes."

"That's..." Kevin groped for a word. "*Asinine.*"

"Yeah, well, after I explained the facts of life to him, Pete agreed."

"He'd better. That is such *bullshit.*"

I laughed. "I'm glad you agree."

"Why wouldn't I?"

"Well – I was kind of a daddy's boy."

"Jamie, we were all daddy's boys. Daddy was all we had. You were just the baby, so you needed him the longest."

"I guess so."

"I know so." I heard voices in the background. "I'd better go. I'll let you know about Pete's friend tomorrow."

"Okay, thanks." I hung up with a smile. In the big brother lottery, I'd come up a winner.

I spent the rest of the afternoon probing the internet again, still without success. Clearly I was going to have to come at the problem from another angle. When I got home, Pete was taking cabbage rolls out of the oven. After dinner, we cleaned up the kitchen together then settled in the living room. I was reading *The Time Traveler's Guide to Medieval England,* and Pete had his laptop open. I assumed he was grading papers, but he set aside the computer after about an hour and asked, "What was your assignment in counseling today?"

That was a surprise. I'd planned to ask Pete about his therapy after his next session, which was Thursday. But he brought it up, so… "My assignment is to ask you to share more about what you're doing in therapy. I told Dr. Bibbins about our conversation last night, and she reiterated that it's important for both of us to remember that we're in this together. I haven't been able to tell her much about what you're doing in therapy, because I don't know."

Pete looked uncomfortable. "It's hard for me – it's so ingrained that everything between a therapist and client is privileged information. Meant to be entirely private." He smiled a little. "I guess maybe psychologists don't make the best clients."

"Like doctors make lousy patients."

"Something like that." He paused – then dropped a bombshell. "I've been thinking… Do you want an open relationship?"

I was stunned to silence for a moment. "*What??* Like cheating with permission? *That* kind of open?"

Pete flinched. "I don't know if I'd phrase it like that, but basically, yeah."

A totally inappropriate picture flashed into my mind – the last time I'd topped anyone, it was my last boyfriend, Scott, and the first thing I thought of was that last time. Of course, I hadn't known it would be the last time. If I had…

I must have had a funny look on my face. Pete asked, "What are you thinking?"

I shook my head to get the picture of naked Scott out of it. "I don't think that's a good idea."

"Why? It would solve the problem. When you needed to fuck someone, you could. No strings attached. And you and I could keep what we have."

I grimaced. "Look. I'm basically monogamous. Serially monogamous in the recent past, true, but monogamous nonetheless.

I've never slept with a guy on the first date. I hate clubbing, and I've never had sex with someone I just met. I know there are a lot of guys that do, and there's absolutely nothing wrong with it, if that's what works for them. But it doesn't work for me. And I know it wouldn't work for you either."

"Why not?"

"Because you flinched when I said cheating with permission. Because you're a one-man man, and you don't like to think about me with other guys. Even if I made sure that you didn't know about it, you'd still know I was doing it, somewhere, sometime, with someone, and you'd resent it. Whether you want to admit it or not, you have some jealous tendencies, and you wouldn't be okay with me having sex elsewhere. Even if you say you would. Even if you *think* you would."

"I don't think I have jealous tendencies."

"I know you don't *think* so. But be completely honest with yourself, and think about how you reacted to Kendall McEwen flirting with me back in January at that rugby match. And think about how you felt when I mentioned Ethan last night. A little jealousy is not a bad thing, but you have to admit it's there."

"Maybe."

Well, that was a start. "And there's another big factor."

"What?"

"Disease. Condoms aren't foolproof."

He blanched. "Oh. I hadn't thought… Boy, that was stupid."

"No, not stupid. You're searching for a solution, and I appreciate that. But an open relationship isn't the answer."

He looked bleak. "Maybe there isn't one."

"No, don't think like that." But I didn't have an answer either.

And, once again, we'd avoided talking about Pete's therapy.

Wednesday, March 20

Pete had given me an iPod for Valentine's Day, loaded with
books and music. It replaced the one that I'd lost in the fire last June,
and I'd begun listening to audiobooks on the bus. This morning it
was Jonathan Kellerman's latest. But I couldn't concentrate on it.
My mind was on what Pete had said the previous evening.

I knew that Pete would never be happy with an open
relationship. I was pretty sure that if we did that, it would eventually
lead to a breakup. And I didn't want that.

But if there was a possibility that Pete would be okay with it,
then should I consider it? I knew that a discreet open relationship
was the answer to sexual incompatibility problems with a lot of
couples. Could it work for us?

I couldn't talk about this to any of my usual confidants. I
wouldn't want my family to know. Liz would think it was a terrible
idea. I wasn't sure what my other friends would think. But I felt like
I needed to talk it over with someone who would at least understand
why I wanted to talk it over. Another gay guy.

So when I got to work, I called a number that I hadn't called
for a while.

When Pete broke up with me the first time we dated to go
back to his old boyfriend Luke, I was unhappy and disillusioned with
relationships. I found a kindred spirit in a guy I'd gone through
library school with named Alex Schuncke. Alex and I had been good
friends in library school and studied together some, but we were both
dating other people and never went out with each other. About the
time Pete broke up with me, Alex's long-time boyfriend left him for
someone else. Alex and I had gotten together to commiserate, and
one thing led to another. We'd ended up dating for about six months,
then decided we made better friends than lovers. We'd both moved
on but had stayed in touch. Alex was a librarian at UC-Irvine, and
we saw each other at conferences and meetings.

Even though Alex and I hadn't been very good at forming a relationship, we'd always been able to talk to each other. We hadn't lost that. When we saw each other at meetings, we'd have a couple of drinks and talk about anything and everything.

Alex was skilled at finding the pros and cons of any situation. It made him indecisive, to be honest, which drove me crazy when we were trying to be a couple. But it was a useful quality to have in a friend.

And there was something else about Alex that would help him understand my situation. He was a survivor of sexual abuse. His had come at the hands of an older cousin, when he was a smaller child, and only involved fondling. He'd overcome it, and we'd had a completely normal sex life. But he'd get where Pete was coming from.

I called Alex's office number, and he answered on the first ring, a bit abruptly. "Library. Schuncke."

"Alex, it's Jamie. Is this a bad time?"

"Jamie! Hi! No, no, it's fine. I was just about to put my fist through my computer monitor, and you've stopped me. How are you?"

I laughed. "I'm fine. But I'd like to have lunch with you one day this week, if I could. My treat."

"Sounds intriguing. Something going on with you?"

"It's a long story. Is there a day that's good for you?"

"Actually, I'm headed that way this morning. I have a meeting at SRLF." The Southern Regional Library Facility was an off-site storage facility for UC Libraries that was on the UCLA campus.

"What time?"

"My meeting's at 10:30. I should be done by 11:30. Want me to come to your office?"

"Yeah. We can grab something on campus."

"Sounds good. See you then."

Alex arrived at my office at 11:35. If there had been an entry for *boy librarian* in the dictionary, it would have used Alex's picture. He was 5'10", skinny, brown hair, brown eyes, average looks. He wore glasses that were always sliding down his nose. He didn't look like a wimp, but he didn't look like someone you'd want on your side in a fight.

But when he smiled, it transformed his face into something beautiful. And he was brilliant. He spoke at least six languages fluently and was conversational in a handful more. He knew something about everything, from string theory to Shakespearean criticism. In library school he'd walked around campus carrying two or three books with him all the time.

We sat on a step and chatted as we ate, catching up on each other's work and families. Then Alex said, "What was it you wanted to talk about?"

I told him what was going on with Pete and me and about the conversation we'd had last night. "My initial reaction was no, that's a terrible idea. But then I thought about it, and wondered if I was wrong. If we could make it work."

Alex pursed his lips in thought. "Have you talked to your counselor about it?"

"Not yet. I don't see her again until Tuesday."

"I know it does work for some couples. But if Pete has a jealous streak, it probably wouldn't work for you guys."

"Yeah. I can imagine the first time I came home after being with someone else. He'd freak out."

"And how would you feel?"

"Like I'd cheated. Even if I had permission, I'd still feel like I'd cheated. I'm just not built for infidelity."

"Because Ethan cheated on you."

"Partly, I guess, and he didn't even cheat on me physically. Just emotionally. And what a betrayal *that* was."

"Mm hm." Alex ate another bite of sandwich. "From what I know, it works best when the couple 'cheats'" – he put air quotes around cheats – "together. You go out to a nice bar, find a nice boy that's open to threesomes, and bring him home with you."

"Oh my God. I can't imagine having sex with someone else while Pete watched. Or vice versa."

"Listen to yourself. You've done nothing except tell me why an open relationship would be a terrible idea for you and Pete. You already know the answer to your question."

"I guess I do. I just needed to talk through it out loud with someone."

Alex smiled. "Glad to oblige. Now I've got a question for you."

"Shoot."

"When did you become so selfish?"

"*What?*" I was confused.

"You heard me. Pete tells you his deepest, darkest secret, that this horrible thing happened to him, and your reaction is how am *I* going to live with this? What about *my* sex life? This is upsetting to *me*. What about just supporting your boyfriend?"

My mouth was hanging open. I closed it and said weakly, "Is that how I sound?"

"Yes." Alex wadded up his napkin and sandwich wrapper then folded his arms and turned to face me. "Pete suffered the worst kind of abuse. He's come a long way, in just being able to function in society, much less have anal sex of any kind. He may eventually be able to do more, or he may not. But that is not up to *you*. There's nothing you can do to speed up the process. It's something he has to do on his own. And a loving, supportive partner who isn't pushing him to do more than he's able is what he needs."

"I *am* supportive. I'm not pushing him to do anything."

"But he feels as if you are. He feels as if he can't satisfy you now, so he's looking for a solution to *your* problem."

"But it's *our* problem."

"No. It's your problem. Tell me this. When you and Pete have sex, is it good?"

"It's beyond good. It's great."

"Does he want to have sex often enough for you?"

"Frequency isn't a problem. Most of the time."

"So you have great sex, as often as you want it."

"Yes."

"And Pete is an awesome boyfriend in every other way."

I saw where he was going with this. "So what do I have to complain about, right?"

"And the answer is nothing. You have *nothing* to complain about. So stop it."

He was right. "God. I've been a total shit."

Alex grinned at me. "*There* you go. Accept that you're a total shit and move on." He stood up and picked up our trash. "I've got to get back to work. Go call your boyfriend."

I stood up and hugged Alex. "Thank you. I knew it was the right thing to talk to you."

He hugged me back. "You're welcome. Pete sounds like a keeper. Don't fuck it up."

"People keep telling me that. I'll try."

He slung his computer bag over his shoulder and began to walk away, then turned and tossed me a last word. "Try harder."

I spent the afternoon looking for more information on Mark Jones, without much luck. I searched using his address, his birth date, his name in connection with Barstow – nothing. He didn't own any property. I searched in the LA Times and the Barstow Desert Dispatch. I searched the UCLA alumni association website. Nothing.

I was running out of ideas.

When I got off the bus that evening, I stopped by a florist on Wilshire and picked up some flowers. Nothing extravagant, just a bunch of daisies – but I still had Alex's admonition ringing in my ears, and I wanted to do something. I'd made a pledge to myself a few months ago to be more romantic, and that had gone by the wayside lately.

I opened the door and heard Pete yell from upstairs, "Be down in a minute."

I yelled back, "Okay," and went to the kitchen to find a vase.

I was arranging the daisies on the kitchen counter when Pete came down. His face lit up. "What's the occasion?"

"No occasion, just an impulse."

He grinned, ridiculously pleased. "I love it."

I really needed to do this more often.

We had a nice evening. Good dinner, pleasant conversation – I didn't want to ruin it. I wanted to further digest what Alex and I had talked about before I brought it up with Pete. Since his therapy was tomorrow, I figured we could talk tomorrow evening.

After dinner we watched a movie – *Forbidden Planet* was on TCM – then went to bed. I was drifting off to sleep when Pete said quietly, "Jamie?"

"Hm."

"Last night, when I asked you about an open relationship, at first you had an odd look on your face. What were you thinking?"

Oh boy. "I had a flashback to the last time I'd topped."

"Oh." A moment of silence. "That was Scott."

"Yeah."

"You and he were compatible."

"Yeah." I wasn't going to offer any more information than I had to.

"You were together a pretty long time."

"About fourteen months."

"What was he like?"

Okay, this was getting weird. "Why?"

"I never met him. I'm just curious."

There was something else going on here, but I didn't know what it was yet. "He was – his music came first." Scott was a cellist with the LA Philharmonic, a truly gifted musician. "He wasn't particularly interested in my career. He wasn't one to ask about my day. But he was very well-read, so we shared a love of books."

"He sounds kind of selfish."

"He could be. He was definitely more self-centered than other-centered. He would never have made it in a helping profession and he had no desire to teach. But he knew that about himself, and he announced it up front. When I started seeing him, I'd just come out of a relationship with a clingy guy – remember how Eric was? – and I thought it would be nice to be with a guy who didn't have to know every detail of everything I did."

"I remember. Eric *was* clingy."

"Beyond reason."

"What did you do with Scott? I know he didn't like the outdoors."

"No. Or sports. But we did a lot together. I went to all of his concerts and recitals and other gigs. I enjoyed listening to the music, and I met a lot of interesting people. We went to readings at bookstores. We went to lectures, sometimes, if someone we wanted to hear was speaking at one of the universities. We went to the movies, film festivals in particular. We went to other concerts if it was someone we both wanted to hear, and sometimes we went to clubs that had music."

"He was educated?"

"Oh yeah. Bachelor's from Juilliard, master's from Eastman."

"Eastman?"

"Eastman School of Music, University of Rochester. Top-rated music school in the country."

"What did your family think of him?"

"They pleasantly tolerated him. Liz liked him. We ate out a lot, but Scott had taken several cooking classes in Asian cuisines. That's another thing we did, we took a cooking class together once.

Anyway, he and Liz would get in his kitchen and cook together. We had some awesome meals."

"He lived in West Hollywood, right?"

"Yeah. He had a very posh condo. It was smaller than this place, but it had a gourmet kitchen."

"And he taught you about clothes. How to recognize designers."

I chuckled. "Yeah. He was a sharp-dressed man."

"Was he – like – out and proud?"

"Yeah. It's not a big deal in the music world."

"No, I guess it wouldn't be."

"He was an activist, at least financially. He tried to only spend money at gay-owned or gay-friendly businesses. He donated money to several gay-related causes." I raised up on my elbow so I could look at Pete. "Why do you want to know all this? Why now?"

"I – his name has come up a few times, and – he was your last, before me, and I didn't know anything about him. I was curious."

"Just curious?" I thought there was more to it.

"Yeah. And…" He trailed off. He seemed to be thinking about how to word whatever he was going to say. "Last night you mentioned jealousy. Monday night you were talking about Ethan. I was thinking that if I knew more about your exes, especially – um – their less stellar qualities, that I might not feel threatened."

"Is that how you feel? Threatened?"

"Not entirely. I mean, I feel pretty confident that you won't pack up and go back to one of them. But I don't know much about any of them. I thought if I knew more, I might be less inclined to be jealous."

"In that case, here's what you need to know about Scott. He could be selfish, he put his career first, he hated the outdoors, and he did not tolerate illness well. I had a lot of trouble with my asthma that spring – a year ago – and he didn't want to hear it. He broke up with me while I was in the hospital, remember?"

"I remember."

"Does that make you feel better?"

"Yeah. I think it does."

"Good." Since Pete was in a talking mood, I decided to resolve the open relationship issue. "Listen, I was thinking about the open relationship idea some more today, and I do not think that's a good idea."

"Well, you pretty much said so last night – why?"

"Because I don't want that. And I don't believe that you want it. I think we should agree that we're going to be monogamous."

"Okay. I agree." He sounded relieved. "But promise me that if you ever change your mind, you'll tell me."

"Of course I'll tell you. But I can't imagine that happening." I rolled on my side and reached out to him. "You are enough for me. I love you. Period. I want you. No one else."

I could almost feel him smiling. "Oh yeah? Talk is cheap – how about some action?"

Thursday, March 21

I was between the bus stop and the library when Kevin called. "Sorry I didn't get back to you yesterday, but we got busy. The ME released the body. The official answer is that it was suicide."

"Okay, thanks for letting me know."

"One other thing – his blood alcohol level was .17."

"Oh. So his judgment was impaired."

"Yeah, unfortunately. I told the family so you can pass that on to Pete if you want. Talk to you later."

When I got to the office, I checked the LA Times website. Mark's obituary had finally appeared.

> **JONES, Mark D., 38, of Westwood, passed away suddenly on March 17, 2013. He was born in Dayton, Ohio and moved to California as a child. He was a graduate of Barstow High School and UCLA, and was an actuary with AIG. He is survived by his partner, Hunter Mitchell, his mother, Elaine Smith (Wendell), his father, Lloyd Jones (Brenda), his sister, Marcia Leider (Charles), and his nieces, Molly and Emma. A memorial service will be held Friday, March 22, 2013, at 9:00 am at Founders Metropolitan Community Church. Graveside service will follow at Forest Lawn – Glendale.**

I texted Pete with the information. He didn't teach on Fridays. He did have office hours from 10-11, but skipping that wouldn't be a problem. I requested a personal day from my supervisor, which she granted. Theoretically I could work half a day tomorrow, but I wanted to be available in case Pete needed me.

Now I had some more information about Mark to work with. I went to AIG's website and couldn't find anything about individual employees. I didn't expect to, but it was worth a try.

Next I went back to LinkedIn. I had created a LinkedIn profile a couple of years ago after hearing about it at a conference, but had never used it. I didn't see the point of it unless you were actively looking for work, which I wasn't. But it was coming in handy now. I logged in and searched for Mark D. Jones AIG and found him.

His profile didn't tell me a lot. He'd worked his way up at the company, with titles hinting at increasing levels of responsibility on his résumé. He'd graduated from UCLA with honors. He was involved in several charities. It was very professional, and not the least bit indicative of why Mark might have killed himself.

At the reference desk, I filled Liz in on my lack of progress. She said, "He sounds like you."

"How so?"

"You have no online footprint either, other than your work. No Facebook page, no Twitter account, no blog or personal web page. Any Google search for you would bring the searcher right here to UCLA, and that would be it."

She had a point. "How am I ever going to find anything, then?"

"Maybe you need to talk to the boyfriend."

"How am I going to do that? I can't just call the guy and say, 'Hey, my boyfriend wants to know why your boyfriend hung himself.'"

"No, *duh*, you're going to the funeral tomorrow, right? Express your condolences and let the boyfriend talk. Maybe Pete can ask a few carefully worded questions. You'll probably be able to speak to anyone in the family you want."

I was about to respond when Clinton arrived. He usually smiled at us, but today he was solemn. "The word of the day is *malversation*." He bowed and walked away.

Liz said, "Is that related to conversation?"

I looked it up. "No. It means corrupt behavior in a position of trust."

"Huh. Does that mean anything to you?"

"No. He must have picked something at random today."

But I was wrong.

The more I thought about it, the more determined I became to take Alex's advice. At dinner that evening, I said, "I want to apologize to you."

Pete looked surprised. "For what?"

"For reacting the way I did to the news of your abuse. For selfishly worrying about what it meant for me when I should have just been supportive of you. I know it was an awful thing. I know how far you've come, and I'm proud of you."

"You can't help the way you feel. And you have been supportive. You've hung in there with me. You could have left."

"I'm not leaving you."

His smile was wide. "I know."

It wasn't until we were in bed that night that I remembered my homework from Dr. Bibbins. "How was therapy today?"

"It was actually productive."

"Yeah, how so?"

"I was telling the therapist about our conversation last night. And she had a suggestion."

"What?"

"You know, the other night, when you were telling me about your grandfather and those other things, those were things I didn't know about you. And I got to thinking about how we find out about each other. How any couple learns about each other. I know information comes to light over time. But it's also good for us to know each other as well as possible. With me so far?"

"Yeah."

"I told the therapist about that, and here's her idea. Every night, when we go to bed, we get to ask each other one thing. And the other has to give an honest answer."

"It can be anything?"

"Yes. Anything from favorite color to – well, I don't know, but something a lot more serious than that."

"I already know your favorite color." Blue.

He whacked my arm lightly. "That was just an example, ya goof. What do you think?"

"I think it sounds good. If you're sure you want to do it."

"Yes, I'm sure. And you can go first."

"Now?"

"Why not?"

"Okay." I took a deep breath, because I'd wanted the answer to this particular question since last Christmas. "Why didn't you ever tell Luke about your abuse?"

He was silent for a moment. I doubted he was expecting that. "Boy, you took me seriously when I said it could be anything."

"Well, I already know your favorite color."

That got a little chuckle out of him. "The reason that I never told him is that I couldn't trust him not to tell anyone else. And I also couldn't trust him not to use it against me when we broke up again."

Good God. What a poisonous individual. Why would Pete ever have been with him in the first place? But that was a question for another time. "So I guess that means that you do trust me."

I heard the smile in his voice. "Yeah. I do."

"Thank you. Now it's your turn."

"Okay. Remember last night you told me about Scott, and why I shouldn't be jealous of him?"

"Yeah."

"Tell me why I shouldn't be jealous of Ethan."

Oh, shit. I was having a brain fart. *Say something.* "Because he's 3000 miles away." *Fuck. That was no good.* "Because – because he's a coward." Now I was getting warmed up. "Because he's a spoiled rich kid. And he cheated on me emotionally and left me with rent on a flat that I couldn't afford. Because he's immature. Because -" *Uh oh.* I'd run out of good reasons. "Because he's a Giants fan." *Please let that be enough.*

"My God. A *Giants* fan. It's bad enough living with a Padres fan. I can't *imagine* having to put up with a Giants fan." His tone was teasing.

"Hey, I like the Dodgers fine. Except when they're playing the Padres." I crossed my fingers and asked, "Are those enough reasons?"

"He was a spoiled, immature coward? Yeah, that's enough."

"Good."

But I wasn't off the hook yet. Pete said softly, "But you thought he was the love of your life."

I sighed. "And now I know better. I was immature then too, right? An immature, Padres-loving daddy's boy. When Ethan left it was a bucket of cold water to the face. I woke up and saw him for what he was." I rolled over to face Pete and poked him in the ribs. "And now I'm a grown-up, Padres-loving daddy's boy, and I. Love. You. Forever and ever, amen."

That earned another chuckle. "Amen, you Padres-lover."

I wrapped my arm around his waist and tugged. "Come here, you Dodgers-lover."

Friday, March 22

I was feeling much better about life the next morning. I hadn't realized how concerned I'd been that Pete and I wouldn't be able to make our relationship work. But Alex's figurative slap up the side of my head was exactly what I needed. That, combined with Pete's and my conversation last night – and what came after – had cleared my head, and I was relaxed and happy.

Until I remembered I had a funeral to go to.

It was a beautiful day. There wasn't a hint of smog. The memorial service was at the Metropolitan Community Church, not far from Griffith Park. Pete and I were shown to a row in the center section. They were filling the church methodically from front to back. I looked around the place - I'd never been in here before, although I knew a couple of people that came to church here.

There was a very nicely done - was it called a program, for a funeral? Whatever it was called, someone had put a lot of thought into it. There were pictures of Mark in it, and I studied them. One was a college graduation picture, and his face was shadowed by the cap and tassel. One was with a good looking guy, maybe the boyfriend. The two of them were wearing tuxes and looked happy. There were others, one with a dog, several with groups of friends.

Mark Jones did not look in his pictures like someone who would kill himself. But what did that look like? Could you tell? I should ask my psychologist boyfriend, but now was not the time or place.

Someone was playing classical piano at the front of the church. More people were coming in - it looked like Mark had plenty of friends. At exactly 9:00, the minister stood up. She said the usual words about celebrating Mark's life, then the eulogies began. A woman stood and went to the podium, and Pete whispered, "Marcia." Mark's sister. She thanked everyone for coming and told a few stories from their childhood, one funny one involving Pete and his brother. She said she wished that Mark felt he was able to talk to her. She was in tears when she ended. I reached over and took Pete's hand. When I looked at him, he had tears in his eyes.

A college friend spoke, then a man that had volunteered with Mark at a homeless shelter, then a coworker. It was clear that none of them had any idea why Mark had made his final choice. The boyfriend didn't speak. I figured he was too distraught. God knew I would be.

The minister had some final words to say and thanked everyone for coming. She invited everyone to the graveside service. The coffin was carried out by the pall bearers, then the family came up the aisle. The boyfriend was leaning on another young man – there was some resemblance there; maybe a brother. Two older couples were next – probably Mark's mother with a husband, and his father with a wife. The sister was with her own husband, and trailed by a couple of probable daughters. The daughters looked truly sad, and not simply bored as teenagers sometimes were at funerals. Mark's sister glanced our way then did a quick double take when she saw Pete. Her eyes widened and she slowed. "Are you coming to the graveside?"

Pete whispered, "Yes."

"I'll talk to you there." And she moved on.

The graveside service was at Forest Lawn, the location of the last funeral I'd attended for my former boyfriend Dan Christensen. The service was brief, and the family filed by the coffin one more time. And it was over.

Mark's sister came up to us as we were walking away from the gravesite. "Pete Ferguson. My God, you got tall. Did my mother see you?"

"I don't think so."

"She'll want to say hello." She turned to me and held out her hand. "Marcia Leider."

"Jamie Brodie. I'm Pete's boyfriend."

She looked at Pete with renewed interest then turned back to me. "Brodie. The police detective who came to give me the news was named Brodie."

"He's my brother."

"Well now, that's a weird coincidence." She turned back to Pete. "Actually, I'd heard *you* were a cop."

"I was. I'm teaching now."

"What grade?"

Pete smiled. "College, thank God."

Marcia smiled a little too. "I hear you. I teach middle school."

Pete and I both groaned.

Marcia's smile faded. "Had you seen him recently?"

Pete shook his head. "Not for a year, and then only briefly. I didn't even know he was gay until then."

"He didn't come out to us until about five years ago. I'd suspected, since high school, but never asked him. We weren't a family that shared, you know."

"I know. Neither were we."

Marcia turned to me. "Your brother was very kind. He could have just called, but he came in person. He answered all of our questions, to the extent that he could. But he couldn't answer the most important one. Why?"

Pete asked, "Did you have any idea that something was wrong?"

"No." Marcia teared up again. "I'd just seen him the week before. He seemed fine. His usual cheerful self. He wasn't depressed as far as I knew..." She trailed off.

Pete's voice was gentle. "But he might not have told you if he was."

"No. He never wanted to bother me with what he called 'his little problems.' My mother-in-law has been sick and we've been helping to take care of her. Mark knew that. So he might not have told me if something was bothering him." She wiped her eyes. "Pete, how's your dad?"

"He's fine. Still working."

"No kidding. At Edwards still?"

"Yeah. He talks about retiring but I don't know what he'd do with himself if he did."

"What about Steve?"

"He graduated from CalTech and now he's in Alamogordo, New Mexico."

"Is he married?"

"Divorced."

"He sent us a nice card and made a donation to the LA Gay and Lesbian Center."

"He told me he was going to."

Pete and Marcia fell silent for a moment, just looking at each other. Something passed between them, and Pete said, "He knows."

Marcia said, "You survived."

"My dad did the right thing. He sent me to a good counselor."

I realized the "he" they meant was me. I looked back and forth between the two of them and said, "I didn't realize that anyone outside the family knew."

Marcia said, "It got around. It was best that you moved away, even though Mark missed you guys. People were shocked – until they weren't."

Pete said, "Someone else?"

"Yeah. At least there were rumors. And then the priest left town. I guess they just moved him somewhere else, like they did all those other scumbags."

I asked, "How many years was he there?"

Marcia said, "About six, I guess." She asked Pete, "Were you part of the settlement?"

"No. That would have meant – telling. I'd come a long way, I'd already gotten therapy, I was getting my doctorate and I was in a good place. I didn't want to relive any of that."

"I don't blame you." Marcia hesitated, then asked, "Do you have any contact with Christine?"

"No."

"I don't blame you for that either. Your mother really got shunned in the town, once everyone figured out that it really happened. I know Chrissie took her side."

"She did."

"I haven't seen Chrissie either, since we graduated. She hasn't come back to town at all, and your mother moved away then too." Marcia shook her head slowly. "So much damage."

"It got me away from them, at least. Things were much more stable with my dad."

"Yeah." Then Marcia said, "I always wondered if the same thing happened to Mark."

Pete gasped. "Do you think so?"

"I have no idea. I asked him once and he denied it. But – that year after you moved to Lancaster was a bad one for him. He started lying, he was drinking, his grades dropped, he even ran away once. It was Father Terry that found him and brought him home that time."

"But the rumors weren't about Mark."

"No. Remember Matt Garvey? No one ever came out and said it, but it was his dad that called to complain to the diocese. We didn't find that out until after Father Terry was long gone."

Pete closed his eyes in pain. "Matt was only twelve."

I'd been listening to this in horror. I reached out and took Pete's hand, and he squeezed mine tightly. Marcia said, "I'm sorry I brought all this up. I just wondered if Mark had ever mentioned anything to you about Father Terry."

"No. He didn't."

I said, "If you don't mind my asking, what made you consider that Mark might have been abused? Was it just his behavior that year?"

Marcia said slowly, "No. He really hated the church. He always said it was because of their wealth and hypocrisy. But I wondered." She smiled sadly. "I knew Mark. I always thought he was keeping something from me. And it wasn't like him to maintain such a level of negativity about anything. He was such a positive person." She started to cry again. "I can't believe I'll never see him again."

Marcia's husband walked over to us and put his arm around his wife. She wiped her eyes again and made the introductions. The husband's name was Charlie. He said, "Marcia's mentioned you, from growing up. It's good to meet you."

Pete said, "You too. I'm sorry it's under these circumstances."

"Yeah." Charlie wiped his nose. "Mark was a great brother. Our girls adored him."

Marcia said, "You've got to speak to Mom. If she finds out you were here and didn't say hello, I'll never hear the end of it."

We spotted Mark and Marcia's mother near the driveway. She turned as we walked toward her and came to Pete with her arms open. "Pete Ferguson! It's so good to see you!"

Pete hugged her then introduced me. "This is my boyfriend, Jamie Brodie. This is – um, Mark's mom."

She smiled and took my hand. "Elaine Smith. It's lovely to meet you." She turned back to Pete. "I went from Jones to Smith. Isn't that silly?"

Pete smiled. He said to me, "All the cookie recipes I have are ones that I got from Mark's mom."

"Oh, wow." I smiled at Mrs. Smith. "I have a lot to be grateful to you for, then."

She laughed a little. She and Pete went through the "how is everyone and where are they now" questions again, and she took

Pete's hand in both of hers. "I'm so glad you're doing well." She didn't say anything else, but I knew what she meant.

"Thank you." Pete didn't elaborate either. I knew he was over talking about it.

She nodded at the driveway, where we saw Mark's father departing. "He's handling this very poorly. He didn't react well when Mark came out. I think the wife is partly to blame. She's very concerned with *appearances*."

"Is that the same woman? She looks different."

Mrs. Smith made a sound of disgust. "Oh, no. That's wife number *four*. The other two and I meet for coffee sometimes. They were at least decent human beings. Wife number two is here, as a matter of fact. She loved Mark. This one, I don't even want my granddaughters in her home."

"So Mr. Jones feels bad now that he rejected Mark."

"Bad doesn't begin to cover it." She made a dismissive motion with her hand. "But forget them." She turned to me. "You seem like a lovely young man. Where are you from and what do you do?"

"Thank you, ma'am. I'm from Oceanside, and I'm a librarian at UCLA."

"Oceanside. Did you grow up in a military household?"

"Yes, ma'am."

She nodded. "Good." She put her arm around Pete's waist and gave him a squeeze. "You take good care of this boy."

"Yes, ma'am. I will."

Her smile faded. "I have to go see to Mark's boyfriend. He's having a terrible time. I'm trying to convince him to stay with us for a few days. He doesn't have any contact with his own parents." Her eyes teared up. "How can anyone turn their own child away? How can anyone do what *your* mother did?"

Pete said softly, "I've wondered that myself."

Mrs. Smith hugged Pete fiercely then stepped back. "I'm so glad to see you. We're in the same house. I'd love to have you visit some time." She smiled mischievously. "I'll make cookies."

Pete laughed. "I'd like that."

Mrs. Smith moved away and Pete turned to me. He looked tired. "Ready to go?"

"Yeah." I'd been hoping to speak to the boyfriend, but he didn't look like he was in any shape to talk. Right now he was sobbing on Mark's mother's shoulder.

"Let's go find Dan's grave."

I'd brought flowers. I knew Ben Goldstein, Dan's boyfriend at the time of his death, had made arrangements with Forest Lawn to keep flowers on Dan's grave, but I wanted to make my contribution. We walked along the drive away from the subdued hubbub of Mark's family. Dan's grave was in the next section over. I was glad to see it was well tended. I laid my flowers at the base of the headstone and we stood for a minute. It was peaceful. There were birds singing.

Finally Pete sighed deeply and took my hand. "Okay. Let's go home."

We drove home without saying much. When we got there, Pete dumped his jacket on the loveseat and headed straight for the kitchen. He took down the bottle of Glenmorangie that Kevin and Abby had given us for Christmas, poured two fingers into a glass, knocked it back and poured two more. He gestured at me with the bottle. "Want any?"

"No." I took a beer out of the fridge and took a long drink. "This'll work for me."

Pete went back down into the living room and dropped onto the sofa. He pulled off his tie and tossed it in the direction of his jacket; it fell to the floor. I picked it up, straightened his jacket over the arm of the loveseat and laid his tie over it, then draped my own jacket and tie over his. He waved his glass in the general direction of me and the jackets. "Thanks."

"You're welcome." I sat down beside him, but not touching. I didn't know if he'd want to be touched. "Tough day."

"No shit."

"I didn't realize that anyone else knew what happened to you."

"Like Marcia said, word got around."

"That's bad."

"Yeah." Pete had his closed face on.

"Is there anything I can do?"

"Yeah." He took another drink. "You can find out if the same thing happened to Mark as happened to me."

"Do you really want me to do that?"

"Yeah. I do. I want to know what happened to him. I want to know why he did this. And I want to know if that son of a bitch Terry Moynihan did this to anyone else. And I want to know where he is." He glared at me, his expression fierce. "Will you do that?"

I swallowed hard. "I will."

"Good." He turned his face back to the window.

I had my orders.

Pete drank half the bottle of Scotch and passed out on the sofa for a few hours. I changed into sweats and tiptoed around the house, doing the chores that I'd usually leave for the weekends – cleaning the bathrooms, straightening up the bedroom and office, doing laundry. I found that we had the ingredients to make chili, got the crockpot out and put together a batch. I'd finished all that and settled on the loveseat with my laptop, checking email, when Pete woke up with a grunt. He squinted at me. I'd closed the blinds to keep the afternoon sun out, and it was dim in the living room. "What time is it?"

"Almost 5:30."

"Shit. You should have woken me up."

"Why? You needed that."

He made a noise that neither confirmed nor denied my assertion. "What smells good?"

"Chili. It won't be ready for this evening, though. Are you hungry?"

"God, no. You go ahead and eat." He sat up and groaned. "I feel terrible. Are you working?"

"Checking email."

"I'm gonna take a shower."

"Okay. Need help?"

He waved me off. I went back to my computer. Twenty minutes later he came back downstairs, hair wet, dressed in sweats. I asked, "Feel better?"

"A little."

"Still not hungry?"

"No."

"You should eat something anyway."

"Yeah, okay. Something painless."

I made pancakes. Pete actually revived a little after he ate. We watched TV for a while – an episode of Ancient Aliens was always good for a diversion – and went to bed.

Saturday, March 23

When the alarm went off at 6:30 the next morning, Pete groaned. I turned it off. "Are you awake?"

"Mmph. Yeah."

"Are you up for today, or do you want to stay home?"

"I'm up." But he didn't move.

I got up and pulled the comforter off of him. "Then get out of bed."

He called me a few colorful names under his breath, but he got up. We had work to do.

My best friends from grade school through high school were Alison Fortner, Melanie Hayes, and Robbie Harrison. Ali was my *best* best friend. Her dad worked with mine at Camp Pendleton and we met in kindergarten. Robbie moved to town in third grade, and Mel arrived in fourth grade. We were inseparable until high school, when Robbie went out of zone to El Camino High to play football while Ali, Mel, and I stayed at Oceanside High. As soon as we got our drivers' licenses, Ali and I started a lawn mowing business together and came to dominate the business on the south side of Camp Pendleton. Ali and Mel had grown closer and closer and had become a couple by the time we graduated from high school.

Ali never quit the landscaping business. While Mel and I went to Berkeley, Ali went to UC-Davis for their landscape architecture program. When we graduated, Ali and Mel moved to LA. Mel had been admitted to UCLA's law school, and Ali began a xeriscaping business. Cactus Flower Xeriscaping had started slowly, but Ali now had a booming business with several employees, all women.

Occasionally, Ali needed more muscle for big jobs and recruited her friends to help. She'd asked Kevin, Abby, Pete, and me to help today. We were meeting her at 8:00.

I got Pete in and out of the shower and got aspirin and Coke into him. I fried bacon and made bacon and tomato sandwiches for breakfast. The smell of bacon revived Pete, and he felt well enough to tease me. "We had breakfast for dinner last night, now we're having lunch for breakfast. What's next?"

I laughed. "What's next is that you start cooking again."

We gathered at Ali and Mel's house in Brentwood. Kevin and Abby were already there, drinking coffee and talking to Mel, who was standing barefoot in the driveway. I said, "You're not coming to help us?"

"Ha. I have my own work to do." Mel was in a two-person law practice with Neil Anderson, a Marine buddy of my dad's. They specialized in LGBT issues.

One of Ali's employees arrived with one of the work trucks, and we piled into the two trucks. The home where we were working today wasn't far. It was a huge job – the homeowners were having all the sod removed. Ali and her crew had been here all week but wanted to finish today so they could start creating the drought-friendly landscape on Monday. She'd hired the muscle – Kevin, Abby, Pete, and me – to carry sod all day.

We worked like dogs. I kept an eye on Pete. He looked grim and was drinking a lot of water, but seemed to be doing okay. Kevin had noticed that Pete wasn't saying much and asked me, "What's going on?"

"Mark Jones's funeral was yesterday. It was tough."

"Oh, right."

"I met his sister. She said you were especially kind. She was very impressed."

Kevin grinned. "You should have told her to call my captain."

"Hey, she might." I paused to hurl a chunk of sod into the pickup bed. "Mark's family knew about Pete."

"About – oh. They knew about that?"

"Yeah. The word got around Barstow after Pete moved to Lancaster. And there was suspicion that Pete wasn't the only victim. Another kid's father complained to the diocese and they moved the priest."

Kevin grimaced. "Just like all the others."

"Yeah. And Mark's sister wonders if Mark was a victim."

"Did she have anything to base that on?"

"Nothing concrete – just that Mark had a bad year after Pete moved away. Drinking, falling grades, running away. And it was the priest that brought him home."

"But he never told anyone."

"No. All she has is suspicion." We hurled more sod, and I stopped for a second to stretch my back muscles. "Pete wants me to find the priest."

"Why?"

"He didn't say."

"He's not going to confront him, is he?"

"I don't know, Kev. He asked me to track the guy down, and I'm going to try."

Kevin didn't look happy, but said, "You might start with the Archdiocese of LA website. All of the names and personnel files of the accused priests are there. LAPD's been going through them, but anyone can access them."

"But if no one accused him, his name wouldn't be there, right?"

"No, but it's a start."

I didn't tell Pete about the archdiocese site. I figured I'd see if there was anything to find before I got his hopes up. We were both exhausted when we got home. We ate reheated chili then took a shower together and fooled around a little while we were in there. By the time we were clean and dry we were both ready to collapse. I was drifting off to sleep when Pete said, "We didn't ask each other our questions last night."

"Mm. No." I tried to pull myself back from the edge of sleep. "You go first this time."

"Okay. How did you come out to your family?"

I smiled to myself, remembering. "When I was five years old, I announced at dinner one night that I was going to have a boyfriend when I grew up."

Pete laughed. "You're kidding."

"Nope. Jeff had just started second grade, and he said there was a girl in his class that he liked. My grandfather said he was too young for a girlfriend, and that's when I piped up."

"Wow. What did everyone say?"

"Nothing, for a second. Then my grandfather said, 'Don't be ridiculous. You're not gonna grow up to be one of those *fairies*.' I thought he was talking about Tinkerbell, so I didn't argue with him."

"What did your dad do?"

"Right then, he changed the subject back to Jeff. But after dinner he told me that if I wanted to have a boyfriend, that was fine with him, but it needed to be our secret. Because other people would think it was ridiculous too. And I thought having a secret with Dad was cool, so I didn't tell anyone else."

"So he always knew."

"I guess. I told him again when I was fifteen, and he said, 'I know. You told me when you were five.' And then he gave me a safe sex lecture."

"Heh. I love your dad."

"Yeah, me too. How about you? How did you tell your dad?"

He was quiet for a moment. "The first person I told was the counselor that I started seeing after we moved to Lancaster. I was feeling awful because I thought the abuse was my fault, because I'd been attracted to the priest. The counselor made me see that nothing about the abuse was my fault, and there was nothing wrong with being attracted to other guys. That process took about a year and a half. I was almost sixteen when she asked me if my dad knew that I was gay. I wasn't sure because he and I had never discussed it. She asked if I wanted to have my dad come in with me, so she could moderate the discussion.

"So that's what we did. He handled it pretty well – his concern was that I was still confused about what the priest had done, and the counselor said no. It just so happened that I was gay, but it didn't have anything to do with the abuse. That was what he needed to hear, I guess. And we've never really discussed it again."

"Never?"

"No. The first time I took Luke home with me, I told him I was bringing a guy home, and he said, 'Okay.' And that was it."

"Wow."

"That's just my dad. He's not talkative, not demonstrative. He's told me that he loves me maybe – twice? Three times? And he's not a hugger, like your dad is. But he has told me that he's proud of me over and over. He helped pay for grad school. He's always been there when I needed him. That's more than a lot of guys have from their dads."

"Oh, I know. I hit the PowerBall lottery with my dad. There aren't many like him."

"I know." Pete was quiet for a minute then said, "My therapist has suggested that I start telling the rest of my family about the abuse. I said I didn't have any other family, and she reminded me that I have in-laws."

"Oh." I was surprised. "Do you want to do that?"

"I'm thinking about it. I'd tell your dad first, of course."

"Right. Then – who?"

"Abby. Then Jeff and Val. Then everyone would know."

"You know none of them would think any less of you."

"I know. I just – I'm thinking about it. It's miles outside of my comfort zone."

"If you decide not to, that's fine. It's entirely up to you. It would probably make it easier for Kev if Abby knew. But my dad, Jeff, and Val – if you don't want them to know, they don't have to know."

Sunday, March 24

We slept in Sunday morning – no disruptive phone calls this time. We both groaned as we got out of bed. I was sore in places that I didn't know I had. Pete was moving even more slowly. We managed to get dressed and go to the farmers' market. When we got home I said, "Why don't we drive out and see your dad?"

Pete looked surprised. "Why?"

"Why not? Because he's your dad and we don't spend enough time with him."

"I was going to make stew. We've got all these vegetables."

"Take them out there. You can cook while I talk to your dad about Barstow."

His expression darkened. "Oh."

"I want to ask him if he knows anything about Mark. You said you wanted me to find out. I can't find anything about Mark online, so I have to talk to people. Your dad is one of those people."

"But I'll have to take my pots and everything out there with me."

"So take them."

"Okay." He called his dad to make sure he was home then busied himself gathering what he needed. I got a sturdy cardboard box out of our storage unit and loaded it for him, and we headed for Lancaster.

Pete's dad, Jack, was a machine tool operator, a civilian employee at Edwards Air Force Base. He lived on the east side of Lancaster, in a three-bedroom, two-bath ranch on a dusty lot. No one in this neighborhood had lush sod sucking up precious water. There were a few trees on Jack's lot providing some shade for the deck that ran across the back of the house. Other than that it was desert scrub.

Jack was pleased to see us, if a little nonplussed. He watched in disbelief as we carried Pete's cooking supplies into the kitchen. "What are you boys planning?"

Pete started unloading things onto the kitchen table. "We wanted to see you, but I need to cook. So I'm cooking here."

"What are you making?"

"Stew. I'll give you some for your lunch this week. Or you can freeze it."

"Oookay. I guess this is my lucky day." Jack shot a questioning look my way. I shrugged.

Pete said, "Okay, you two, get out of here so I can cook." He moved the vegetables to the sink and started flinging water as he scrubbed them. Pete was a great cook, but he tended to be messy.

Jack and I moved to the family room, where he settled into his recliner. "Okay, son. I'm delighted to see you, but why are you really here?"

"We really did want to see you. Pete cooks on Sunday, but I told him he could do it here."

He raised an eyebrow. "So this was your idea."

"Not entirely. But it's true, I wanted a chance to talk to you."

"About what?"

"Mark Jones."

His smile faded. "Steve told me what happened."

"Pete wants to know why he did it."

"That's natural. I'm sure Mark's family would like to know that too."

"Yes, sir. We went to the funeral on Friday."

"Ah. How's the family doing?"

"About like you'd expect. I met Marcia and Mrs. Jones, who is now Mrs. Smith. They were really happy to see Pete, and to see that he's doing well. And Marcia suggested that – she thought there was a possibility that Mark might have been abused, too."

Jack's face darkened. "Why does she think that?"

"She said Mark had a bad year after Pete and Steve left. Drinking, lying, running away, bad grades. She said Father Terry brought him home once after he ran away."

"Did Mark ever say anything to her about it?"

"No. But she always thought he was keeping something from her."

Jack rubbed the bottom of his face. "I never met that priest. Didn't want to for fear of what I'd do to him."

"Understandable. You didn't report him?"

"Report him to who? Those clowns were all in that together. And I just wanted to get the boys out of there."

"They *were* all in it together." We brooded together for a moment. "So you never heard anything else about it – about the same priest abusing other kids."

"No. But he would have, wouldn't he?"

"Probably."

Jack said softly, "I have thought about that. Whether I could have saved a kid from that if I'd told someone."

I shook my head. "Marcia said that when someone did complain, they just moved him to another parish. You're right. They were all about covering it up back then. It wouldn't have mattered, it would have just gotten him moved from Barstow sooner."

Jack nodded. "That's what I tell myself."

"It's the truth."

We brooded together for a minute more. Then Jack said, "You should talk to Steve."

"Do you think he might know something?"

"He stayed in touch with a couple of people in Barstow, not just Mark. He might."

Monday, March 25

Monday was going to be a slow day at work. We were between quarters. There were no classes to teach and very few students in the library – just a few dedicated doctoral students slogging away on their dissertations. I had two items on my agenda today. The second was to look at the archdiocese website, but the first was to do a little research of my own.

Scholarly activity – getting papers published, presenting at conferences – was an unfortunate necessity for university librarians. Even though we weren't faculty, we had to jump through the same hoops as faculty did to get promoted. I was up for promotion again next year. I'd presented at one conference each year since I'd been hired, and already this year I'd had a proposal for one paper accepted by a peer-reviewed journal. But I had an idea for another one, and I thought Liz might like to co-author it.

I did a quick literature search to see if there was anything published on the topic. As I suspected, there wasn't. I went to Liz's office and stuck my head in the door. "Want to co-author a paper?"

"On what topic?"

"Librarian involvement in police investigations."

She laughed. "Interesting. What's your idea?"

"I did a preliminary literature search and didn't see anything exactly like it. So we should be able to get it published and present it at a conference without much trouble because it's unique. I've been involved in two investigations now – we could write up my experiences, maybe give some recommendations."

"You could do it yourself."

"I know, but you need to publish, right? And since Jon was the lead on one of those investigations, if we needed his input you could get it."

"Hm. Okay, you're on. Since you're the one with the experiences, I'll do a lit search, make sure there really isn't anything else on the topic."

"Awesome." With that settled, I went to check the archdiocese database.

The list of accused priests was under a "Protecting Children" tab on the archdiocese website. The list was easy to search, as the priests were named alphabetically. They included incidence dates and the number of accusers. They also indicated whether or not an accused priest was deceased.

There was no Terry Moynihan on the list.

This sentence began the paragraph immediately preceding the list of priests: "There are 33 priests who have been accused but whose names do not appear on this list. None of these 33 is the subject of a criminal or civil action." So if no one had ever brought a case against Terry Moynihan, his name wouldn't be here.

Another dead end.

Then it hit me. Barstow wasn't in LA County, it was in San Bernardino County. *Duh.*

I smacked myself in the forehead, then went to the website of the Diocese of San Bernardino. There were two parishes in Barstow, but only one had a website. I shot Pete a text – *Looking for priest – St. Joseph Parish?*

He replied quickly. *Yes.*

There was a section about parish history on the website, but nothing about former priests. The first bishop of the parish had served until 1995. Pete's abuse had occurred in 1989. I Googled the bishop's name; he was still alive at age 80 but had retired.

I found the news story on the San Bernardino diocese's settlement. They had settled 11 cases for $15.1 million in 2007. I read all the documents I could find. No mention of Terry Moynihan. There was also no mention of Matt Garvey, the kid whose father had supposedly blown the whistle on Moynihan. Probably another accusation that didn't generate a legal case.

I found one priest on Google named Terry Moynihan, but he was Australian.

I did a search on Google for "Terry Moynihan" and got 2000 results. Some were women. There were thirteen on LinkedIn alone.

This was getting frustrating. Time to do something else. I pulled up a fresh Word doc and started making notes for my paper.

That evening after dinner I told Pete about my lack of progress. "I'd think that if he was still working, even if he'd resigned in good standing, his name would be out there somewhere. It's like he never existed."

Pete took the news calmly. "If he was asked to resign, they'd make sure that his name stayed out of any discoverable documents. They wouldn't want to give anyone who might sue any ammunition."

"Makes sense. But if that's the case, he'll be hard to find." I told him about my Googling.

"Yeah, I know." He reached over and patted my knee. "You're doing everything you can."

"Your dad didn't know anything more, but he suggested that your brother might. He was Mark's friend too, right?"

"He was. I hadn't thought about that."

"Call him."

Pete had tossed his phone onto the ottoman when we'd settled on the sofa; he retrieved it and punched the right buttons, then put the phone on speaker.

Steve's voice said, "Hey."

"Hey. I have you on speaker so Jamie can hear too. What're you doing?"

"I'm still at work. If I told you what I was doing I'd have to kill you. What's up?"

"Mark's funeral was Friday."

"Yeah. I wish I could have made it."

"Me too. Marcia said she appreciated your donation."

"How are they doing?"

"Pretty well under the circumstances. Marcia said something weird, though. She wondered if Mark was – if he'd had the same issues with the priest as I had."

Steve was silent for a moment. "Mark never said anything about it to her?"

"No. She asked him and he denied it. But she still suspected."

I heard Steve take a deep breath. "He told me."

Pete was stunned. I said, "Oh my God. When?"

"Several months after we'd moved away. Mark came over one weekend during that first summer we were in Lancaster. Remember, Pete?"

Pete's voice was faint. "Yeah. I remember."

"You had a ball game. Dad was down the bleachers a ways talking to a couple of guys he worked with, and Mark and I were by ourselves for a few minutes, and he told me. He made me promise to never tell you."

"Why?"

I said, "Because he figured you'd blame yourself for leaving."

Steve said, "That's it. He was afraid that if you knew, you'd think that if we'd stayed you could have kept it from happening to Mark."

Pete shook his head slowly. "He was right. I would have thought that."

Steve said, "But there's no evidence that had anything to do with his suicide, is there?"

Pete said, "There's no evidence that it didn't."

I said, "That's because there's no evidence at all. The family has no idea why he did it. We didn't get a chance to talk to his boyfriend."

"He didn't leave a note?"

"No. But my brother said that wasn't all that uncommon."

Pete said, "It's fewer than half. In related news, Terry Moynihan seems to have dropped off the face of the earth."

I said, "I've been looking for him online. Marcia said he was at the parish for six years then moved on when someone complained to the diocese. But his name doesn't appear in any of the documents about the settlement. His name doesn't appear anywhere, at least not identified as a priest. I'm thinking he got asked to resign quietly in a way that didn't create a paper trail."

"Sounds logical. Who complained to the diocese?"

Pete answered. "Marcia said it was Matt Garvey's father. But if there was no legal case, there wouldn't be a record of the complaint."

"If he was there six years, then we were both long gone by the time he left. I don't remember hearing anything about it. Or about Matt Garvey."

"No. And Mark was in college by then, too, so he wouldn't have necessarily known either."

I said, "That reminds me. Mark took a year off between high school and college. Steve, do you know anything about that?"

"Um – no. Not that I remember. Pete, you don't remember why he did that?"

"I didn't even know that he'd done it. I thought he'd gone straight to UCLA. It wasn't until I saw him there my freshman year that I found out, and I never asked him why."

Steve said, "Marcia would know. Pete, you could ask her."

"Yeah. I might call her in a few days, see how she's doing and ask her about it. Or – Mark's mom invited me to come see her. She would know."

Pete and Steve talked a bit longer. Pete told Steve about our visit to their dad on Sunday and Steve laughed at the idea of his dad trying to figure out why Pete would show up at his house to cook.

I thought about what Steve had said. So Marcia's suspicions were right, and Mark had been abused by the priest. But that may not have had anything to do with his reasons for killing himself.

When Pete hung up, I asked, "Are you going to tell Mark's family about his abuse?"

"No. Unless they ask me again directly. Knowing that now would only make them feel worse. I do want to visit Mark's mom, though. And it would give me a chance to show you where I grew up."

"Wow. I'm pleased that you want to do that. And that you feel like you're able to go back there."

Pete shrugged. "I haven't been back there for 24 years. My female relatives are long gone. And I was happy there as a small child, before my parents' marriage started going bad. I'd like to show it to you."

"I'd love to see it."

We showered together, which led to sex in the shower – so easy to clean up afterwards! – and falling into bed naked. Neither of us were used to sleeping in the nude, but we were trying it more often. Even though I wasn't in rugby shape any more, I'd still kept my muscle definition in my legs thanks to running and hiking, and Pete was tracing the outlines of my quadriceps with a finger. "Ready for your question?"

"Yep."

"Why rugby?"

"Ah. I started it because a couple of kids at school played, and it looked fun. Not boring like soccer. I kept it up because I was better at it than baseball, and because it had such a reputation as a rugged sport. No one would suspect a rugby player of being gay. And no one did."

"Heh. At least until Gareth Thomas came along."

"Right."

"What position did you play in baseball?"

"Shortstop. I was a good fielder but I couldn't hit the curve ball."

Pete chuckled. "The downfall of many a potential major leaguer."

"Yeah. Ready for your question?"

"Lay it on me."

"I want you to be completely, completely honest and tell me one thing that you'd change about me if you could. One thing that drives you nuts."

He chuckled. "I don't know that I'd change this, because it does benefit me, but – you're almost too clean. Not you personally, I mean, but how clean you keep the house. You're a little obsessive about it."

"Oh. Well – my grandfather taught me to clean. He didn't make me scrub the grout with a toothbrush, but he was almost that exacting. He said my wife would appreciate it one day." I poked him in the ribs. "Are you telling me he was wrong?"

Pete laughed. "I'm sure if you had a *wife*, she would. I guess my standards aren't as high as the Marines. But sometimes I think – like, when you picked my tie up off the floor last Friday – oh, just leave it for now. But you never do."

"It's also because of my asthma. If dust doesn't accumulate, it can't give me an attack."

"That's true."

"Do you want me to be messier?"

"No, I just don't want you to be uptight about it. I want you to be able to relax without having to pick up every dirty sock first."

"Okay, the next time you think, 'Oh, just leave it for now,' say it out loud. We'll see if I'm capable of leaving a sock on the floor."

"Deal." Pete snuggled against me and we both fell asleep almost immediately.

I dreamed that I came home from work and opened the door to find mountains of dirty socks throughout the house.

Tuesday, March 26

Dr. Bibbins picked up her notebook. "As we discussed last week, today is our final session. We've come as far as we're able without Pete's participation. Let me emphasize, if you can convince him to begin couples counseling, I'll be happy to see you both. Or, if at any time you feel like you need therapeutic support again, call me. Once a client, always a client."

"Thank you. I appreciate that."

"I don't think either of you will achieve your relationship goals until you work on them together."

"I agree. But I've been doing some thinking about our goals." I told Dr. Bibbins about my conversation with Alex, and my discussions with Pete over the past week.

She said, "Those are valuable insights. Do you believe you can maintain that determination, to let Pete dictate the terms of your sex life?"

"I think so. What Alex said – that was a real eye-opener. I'm not going to forget that."

"That's fine, but the compatibility issues aren't going away. Tell me what you're going to do on your own to deal with that. We've talked about strategies."

I had a tuna salad sandwich today; I swallowed the last bite and counted on my fingers. "One. I'm going to exercise more. I'm going to join the Santa Monica Y. Their schedule is far more accommodating than the pool at UCLA."

"You like to swim?"

"I grew up in the ocean. I swim like a fish. I love it."

"Does Pete swim?"

"He can swim, but it doesn't come as naturally to him."

"Will he want to join with you?"

"He might. He's been talking about wanting to work out more. He could use the gym while I'm swimming."

"If you suggest that he join too, he won't feel as if he's being excluded."

"Right. And that would go along with my second strategy, which is to work on strengthening our relationship in other ways."

"Yes. Examples?"

"I made a list." I'd tucked the slip of paper into my lunch bag; now I pulled it out. "Take a class together, like…I don't know…plumbing or something. Look for a conference we can attend together, maybe something on academic publishing. Spend more time with Pete's family. We spend lots of time with mine, but not so much with his, and his dad is closer to us in Lancaster than mine is in Oceanside. And I'd like to visit his brother in New Mexico, too, instead of just waiting to see him when he comes here."

Dr. Bibbins was nodding. "That all sounds excellent. But you're forgetting something big."

I was? "I am?"

"Yes. You said in February that Pete told your brother about his abuse, so you'd have someone else to talk with. It was one of his Valentine's Day gifts to you. Have you been doing that?"

"Oh! No, I haven't. I've been talking to you, and I got busy with work – I never got around to it."

"Don't you think you should?"

"Absolutely. I'll call him as soon as I leave here."

"Excellent." She stood up and held out her hand. "Good luck, Jamie. If you need to see me again, just call."

"Thank you. I will."

I called Kevin as I walked back to my office. He was in a rush, but said he could meet me for lunch tomorrow. When I got home that evening, Pete was chopping bell peppers. I eased into the kitchen and kissed him. "Whatcha making?"

"Stir fry."

"Can I help?"

"Sure." He reached into the refrigerator and pulled out a bowl. "You can peel the shrimp."

I moved to the other side of the sink and started peeling. "How was your day?"

"Fine. Uneventful. You?"

"It was fine. I had my last session with Dr. Bibbins."

He glanced at me but didn't stop chopping. "Really."

"Yeah. She says we've done as much as we can individually."

"Meaning?"

"Meaning she thinks we should have couples counseling. But until then, she's given me some things to do."

He frowned. "I don't know about couples counseling."

"I know that. But I don't know why. What have you got against it?"

His face didn't betray anything, but he chopped a little harder. "I tried it once before."

Oh, no. "With Luke?"

"Yes."

"Pete. I'm not Luke."

"Believe me, I'm well aware of that."

"And you'd be seeing a different therapist."

"I know."

"So you won't consider it."

"Not right now." He scraped the chopped vegetables into the wok. "What are these other things you're supposed to do?"

I sighed. "One of the things she suggested is to get more exercise. I've always wished I had more time to swim, so I was thinking I'd like to join the Y. Their lap pool is open early in the morning and late into the evening. And you've been saying you want to work out more – if you didn't want to swim, you could go to their gym while I was swimming."

He thought about that for a minute. "You're not talking about every evening, right?"

"No. Probably twice during the week, once on the weekends. It would give us something to do in the early morning if we can't run for some reason, or if we do run in the morning, we could go to the Y in the evening."

"Would we have to get individual memberships?"

"I don't know. We could try to talk them into a family membership."

Pete turned the heat on under the wok and moved the cutting board with the vegetables to the side. He reached into the bowl to help peel the last of the shrimp. "This extra exercise is supposed to work off frustration, I'm guessing."

"That's the idea. Plus, I do miss swimming. Since I left Berkeley, I've never gotten to swim as much as I used to. So this is a two birds, one stone deal. And it's better for us than sitting around here watching TV in the evenings."

"True." Pete patted his abs. "I'll be forty before you know it…"

"And you're in great shape. This will just help us stay that way."

"Yeah, right. You're such an optimist." But he kissed me, then swatted me on the ass. "Get out of here and let me cook."

After dinner we both read for a while. Pete was reading a psychology journal. I was in the mood for something light and was reading a book that I'd downloaded for free onto my Kindle app, a male-male romance with a mystery subplot. The farther I got into the book, the more I realized I'd gotten what I paid for. The subplot was thin and implausible and the sex scenes were ridiculously over the top. Halfway through the fifth one – within the space of one and a half chapters – I actually laughed out loud. Pete looked up. "I didn't think you were reading anything funny."

"It's not supposed to be. It's a sex scene."

"Sex can be funny."

"Yeah, but the sex in this book is supposed to be hot. Listen to this. And this is all from just one scene. 'Man lance, turgid magnificence, silken steel, throbbing member, hot torpedo, huge appendage, powerful manhood, aching staff, purple sheath, aching sex.'"

Pete was laughing. "Oh my God! Stop!" He grinned and tossed aside his journal. "How 'bout I show you my turgid magnificence?"

Afterward we took a shower together and fell into bed. We snuggled together, Pete draped over my chest. He said, "Ready for your question?"

"Yeah."

"I know about your grandfather now, but I don't know about your grandmother. Or your other grandparents. Tell me about them."

"My dad's mother died when he was in Vietnam. She was out in her garden on a really hot day and keeled over with a heart attack. She was a heavy smoker."

"Oh. So that's how your grandfather was available to help raise you all."

"Yeah. As for my mom's parents – they fought my dad for custody after my mom died. They were determined to get us away from him, even though none of us knew them at all."

"Did they think your dad was unable to take care of you?"

"I don't know. My grandfather – Dad's father – said that they were completely unable to accept the fact that my mom was gone. So they wanted us not for our sakes, but for theirs."

"He was probably right. So you never met them?"

"I met them twice. I guess I was around six the first time, and nine the second. Every summer we'd go to South Carolina to see my dad's family for two weeks, and twice when we were there my mom's parents came to visit."

"That must have been uncomfortable."

"Yeah. We didn't know them, so – we were polite to them, but it was probably clear to them that we weren't interested. We knew what they'd tried to do. And my grandparents had no idea how to talk to little boys. They were a good bit older than my dad's parents. So it was awkward. I remember when my grandmother saw Jeff that first time she burst into tears."

"Jeff looks the most like your mom, I guess."

"Yeah. Obviously Kevin and I look a lot like Dad, so she wasn't as interested in us."

"Was your mom an only child?"

"Yeah."

"And they lived on the east coast?"

"In the eastern time zone, at least. Huntington, West Virginia. I've been there once. Ethan and I went over spring break when we were in college. My grandparents were gone by then and I wanted to see where the other half of my roots was."

"So they're both gone?"

"Yeah. If they were alive they'd be over 100 now. Okay, your turn. Grandparents."

"Oh boy." Pete chuckled softly. "Well, first, the two sets of grandparents hated each other. *Hated* each other. So things always had to be arranged so they didn't cross paths."

"Oh wow."

"Yeah. After my parents got divorced that part got easier. Our dad's parents would see us when we were at our dad's. Our mom's parents had retired to Arizona and only came for holidays. My dad's parents lived in Victorville. When we were going to see my dad, his parents would come pick us up at our mom's, since they were closer to Barstow. Then they'd drive us to Dad's. Then after Steve and I moved in with Dad, we never saw our mother's parents again. They may still be alive, for all I know."

"They chose sides."

"Yeah. But our dad's parents were great. My grandfather was a crusty old coot, but he was hilarious. And my grandmother was Uncle Arthur's sister, so she was fine with me being gay."

"What happened to them?"

"My grandfather died when I was in college. He was a smoker too, and he had lung cancer. And my grandmother died just before I met you. She'd had rheumatic fever as a child, and had a bad heart valve, and it gave way on her. The doctors had wanted to replace it, and she refused. She didn't like hospitals."

"I wish I'd known them. I know I only met Uncle Arthur a couple of times, but I liked him."

"He liked you too. He'd be happy to know you were living with me in his house."

"You think so?"

"Mm hm." Pete snuggled against me and tucked his head under my chin. "I know so."

Wednesday, March 27

It was the first day of spring quarter. There was a buzz of energy in the air – not as palpable as with the start of the fall quarter each year, but still present. My class didn't meet until Monday night, but the students could access the course website as of this morning, and they'd find a simple assignment waiting for them. I'd already gotten an email from a student with a question, the answer to which was right there in the syllabus. I was composing a reply to that effect when she called.

There was at least one every semester – a needy student who took more time than the others combined in terms of hand-holding. I hoped she was the only one.

I'd just hung up the phone when James Wygant, our circulation supervisor, came to my door. "Dr. Brodie, I want you to meet our new circulation work-study students for spring. Grace Cavender and Alicia Kwan."

I stood and shook hands with the ladies. Alicia Kwan was a chubby young woman with a ponytail. She gave me a friendly grin. Grace Cavender was of medium height and medium build with medium brown hair. She gaped at me like – almost in wonder. *What was that about?* "It's nice to meet you both. Welcome to YRL."

James ushered them along to Liz's office. I heard them being introduced, then they walked back past my door. Grace gazed in and gave me a little wave as she passed.

Uh-oh. I didn't have time to worry about her, though. I had work to do before I met Kevin for lunch.

Kevin got to the plaza right on time. We found a free piece of concrete and sat, and Kevin doled out burgers and fries from In 'N Out. "So. What's going on?"

"My counselor discharged me, and said I should spend more time talking to you. So here you are."

"And I even bought lunch."

"And you even bought lunch."

"What do you want to talk about?"

"Well… Remember back in February you said you didn't want to hear about my bedroom issues?"

"Yeah?"

"Yeah. As it turns out, if we can't talk about that, it's not going to be all that helpful."

Kevin scratched his nose and looked off into the distance. "I was afraid it might come to that."

"It's up to you. If you really don't want to hear it, I understand. And I promise not to get into a lot of detail."

He gave me a sideways look. "Can I reserve the right to tell you if it's too much detail?"

"Yep."

He took a long drink of Coke. "Okay. Lay it on me."

"Do you know about tops and bottoms?"

"I'm familiar with the concept."

"Some guys have preferences one way or the other, but a lot of guys, when they're with a partner, like to take turns. I'm one of those guys. Everyone I've ever dated before has been one of those guys. Until now."

"Even *Scott?*"

"Yes, even Scott. Focus, please. Back when we first started seeing each other, the first time, Pete told me that he never bottomed. Ever. Which at the time was not a big deal, since we weren't living together and only managed to sleep together a couple of nights a week anyway. And of course I had no idea why."

"But this time is different."

"Yeah. This time we're together every night. And again, last summer it was fine, but then in the fall I started getting kind of tired of it. I figured Pete just didn't like it for some reason, and I could eventually change his mind. I was still trying to decide how to approach that right up until Christmas Eve."

"But now you know why he won't do it that way."

"Yeah. And I can't ever ask him to. If he ever decided he wanted to try it, that'd be great, but that would have to be entirely on his own. And chances are good he won't ever do that."

"So the problem you're having now is that you're tired of having sex the only way that Pete wants to have it."

"That's part of it. I mean, there are other things we do that – um – don't involve anyone bottoming, shall we say? And those are fine, because we're equal in those. But not only am I tired of being a bottom, I miss being a top. Think about it – what if someone told you that you'd never have penetrative sex again?"

"*Shit.*"

"Exactly. So I went to the counselor to get help with handling the frustration of that. And also to be able to talk through how I was feeling about Pete's revelation in general, because at the time you didn't know."

"Right. So the counselor's done everything she can for you."

"Individually, yes. She thinks we'd benefit from couples therapy, but Pete's not ready for that."

"But he's seeing a therapist."

"Yeah, but it's psychotherapy. As I understand it, that's only useful for figuring out yourself. It's not that helpful for relationship issues."

"So am I your only hope?"

I laughed. "No, Obi-Wan. For now, I'm also going to start swimming again, to burn off some excess energy."

Kevin finished off his fries. "What are you looking at, long term? Is anything going to change?"

I sighed. "I don't know. Do I think Pete will ever let me top him? No. Although saying that out loud creates despair in my soul…"

"So don't say it out loud anymore."

"Ha ha. What I would like is to get him into couples therapy, and see if we could work on – um – this may be getting into the TMI zone for you."

Kevin sighed. "Go ahead."

"Well, right now, Pete won't do *anything* that reminds him in any way of what happened to him. Including a lot of different positions, even if he's still the top. He'll only do it one way. If we could at least get to the point where we could vary our positioning, that would be helpful."

"It's that bad for him?"

"Kev. Right now he can't even *hug* me from behind."

"*Damn.*"

"Exactly."

Kevin checked his watch and gathered up our trash. "I need to go. Listen, Abby's spending the weekend with her sister, the one who just had twins. Why don't you guys come over Friday night? We can cook out, watch a ball game."

"Sounds good. I'll talk to Pete."

"Cool." He gave me a friendly smack on the shoulder. "Hang in there, short stuff."

Thursday, March 28

Early Thursday morning I presented my first research instruction session of the spring quarter. As I was passing the circulation desk on the way back to my office, a voice said, "*Hi*, Dr. Brodie."

I glanced at the desk. Grace Cavender was standing behind it, beaming at me. I must have looked puzzled, but said, "Hi," and kept going.

About fifteen minutes later I got an IM from Connie at circulation. *Coming to see you.*

OK.

A couple of minutes later, Connie breezed into my office and closed the door. "You're in trouble."

She was laughing, so I didn't think I was in too much trouble. I was wrong. "How so?"

"Miss Grace Cavender, work-study student *médiocre*" - she used the French pronunciation - "has a crush on you, mister."

"Oh, God. Did you explain the facts of life to her?"

"I did. She seems to be laboring under the delusion that gay men just haven't met the right woman yet."

"Oh, *hell* no. Call her off, Connie."

"I'm trying. But let me tell you, the girl's favorite books are the Love Comes Softly series."

"What's that?"

"Historical Christian romance fiction. She thinks the fact that you're a history specialist is a sign from God."

I groaned. "She's an undergrad, right? Tell her how old I am."

"I did. She thinks the age difference is just right."

"Tell her I'm not a virgin. Tell her I hath lain with men. And I *liked* it."

Connie had never really stopped laughing but that got her laughing even harder. So much so that there was a knock on the door and Liz stuck her head in. "What the hell's going on in here?"

I waved her in frantically. "Get in here. Emergency strategy session."

"About what?"

Connie told her. By the end of it Liz was laughing too. "This is *great*."

"This is the *opposite* of great. What's the matter with you? I need a plan to get this girl off my case."

"Oh, c'mon." Liz wiped her eyes. "Haven't you ever had to deflect a woman's attention before?"

"No!"

Connie was still giggling. "You've fended off twinks before, right? How different can it be?"

"Not *Christian* twinks. If I ask her nicely to stop and she doesn't, I can't tell her to fuck off."

"Sure you can. Maybe she'll be so offended she'll never speak to you again."

"I also can't tell her that because I can't say that to anyone at work. And I'm sure as hell not going to have any interaction with her away from this building."

Liz said, "I think your best bet is just to be monotonous. Everything she says to you, say, 'I'm gay. I'm gay. I'm gay.' Over and over. 'What's your favorite color, Dr. Brodie?' 'I'm gay.' 'How's this weather we're having, Dr. Brodie?' 'I'm gay.' 'Where are the American history books kept, Dr. Brodie?' 'I'm gay.' Maybe she'll give up."

Connie said, "I don't know. She's pretty sold on you."

"Well, unsell her! Maybe that what you need to say over and over. 'He's gay. He's gay.'"

"I can try." Connie got up. "I just thought I'd better warn you. She hasn't talked about anything else since yesterday except for you." She opened my door and pointed to the sign beside it that said

No Perfume or Cologne! Asthma! "And I'd get that printed again in nice bright colors. Today she's drenched in White Shoulders."

Liz rolled her eyes. "Oh my God. My grandmother wore that. I didn't know they still made it."

"My grandmother still wears it." Connie waved. "Good luck."

I begged. "Liz. You have to help me."

She grinned at me. "I think it's sweet."

"You do not. Stop it. What am I gonna do?"

"First, get some pictures of Pete in here. Half-naked, if possible. If that doesn't work, get Clinton to speak with her. He'd have the right vocabulary."

"I have a picture of Pete in here." It had been taken on a hiking jaunt up at Eagle Rock. We had our arms around each other, the ocean at our backs. It was my favorite picture of us.

"Yeah, but it's tame. And one isn't enough. I recommend as many as possible."

"Okay. I'll find more. I'll take a bunch and print them tonight if I have to."

"Good. Am I allowed to tell Jon about this?"

"No!"

She laughed. "Really, didn't you have girls hitting on you in high school? Or college? As cute as you are?"

"I always had Ali and/or Mel to deflect the girls in high school and college."

She looked surprised. "In college, too?"

"Yeah, Mel went to Berkeley with me. Ali was at Davis. She'd come down on the weekends and Ali, Mel, Ethan, and I would all go out together. It kept us out of trouble."

"Maybe you need to ask Ali or Mel how to fend off a woman's attentions. *Grace*-fully."

"You're *so* funny. Can you sue a work-study student for sexual harassment?"

Liz left my office laughing harder than ever.

Our reference shift began at 1:00. By the time Clinton appeared at 1:30, Grace had walked by the desk four times, practically batting her eyes at me each time.

Clinton said, "The word of the day is *philter*." He bowed, but didn't walk away.

Liz had already been giggling because of Grace. Now she looked the word up and immediately began to laugh even harder. I said, "What?"

She tried to speak and started to laugh again. She pushed her monitor screen in my direction and pointed to the definition. I read it out loud. "'A potion, charm or drug supposed to cause the person taking it to fall in love.' Oh, no. Clinton. *No*."

He smiled benignly.

"Clinton. I'm serious. How do I convince this girl that I'm not interested?"

"I believe that polite persistence is your best strategy. Eventually she will tire of the pursuit and turn her attentions elsewhere." He turned serious. "I have another word for you. *Dispositive*."

Liz was still incapacitated with laughter, so I looked it up. "Involving or affecting disposition or settlement." I stared at Clinton. "Settlement? As in – financial settlement? As in diocese of San Bernardino?"

"Indeed."

I leaned back in my seat, amazed that I hadn't considered this. "You could help."

"Possibly."

Liz was paying attention now. "Help with what?"

"Help find a priest. Probably an ex-priest by now. His name is Terry Moynihan. He served in San Bernardino in the late 1980s to early 1990s."

Liz asked, "Why are you looking for him?"

This was getting into dangerous territory. I said, "Pete thinks he may have something to do with his friend's suicide."

Clinton bowed again. "I will do my best. It will take some time."

"Whatever you can find out would be helpful."

Clinton nodded and walked away. I watched him go, thinking. Clinton had been a monk, not a priest, and had served at an abbey in Oregon. But he would know better than anyone how to find Terry Moynihan.

If and when he did, what would Pete do?

I decided not to tell Pete about Clinton's offer yet. I did tell him about Grace and his reaction was the same as Liz's – uncontrollable laughter. "Oh boy. You're in trouble."

"Why does everyone think this is so funny? This is so *not* funny."

"Aw, c'mon. Where's your sense of – whimsy?"

"*Whimsy?* Where's your sense of jealousy when I really need it?"

"Okay, okay. What do you want me to do?"

"Tomorrow's Friday. Come take me to lunch."

"I'll do better than that. I'll drive you to work and stay all day. I have plenty of reading and research I can do. That way we'll have the car with us to go to Kevin's."

"Don't you have office hours?"

"I changed them. I have an extra hour on Thursday now. No students ever came to see me on Friday."

"Oh. Well, good. You spending the day is a great idea."

"And this weekend we'll take some pictures."

"Sounds like a plan."

"So here's my question for the evening. Have you ever kissed a girl?"

I made a face. "No, gross. Cooties. Did you?"

"Yeah, in college."

"Ah. You weren't out to anyone but your family."

"No. And the girls liked me because I didn't try to paw them. I was a perfect gentleman."

I laughed. "You must have broken a few hearts."

"Nah. I always made it clear I wasn't in the market for a relationship. If some of them chose not to believe that – not my problem. But I never had any trouble."

"Did you like it? Kissing girls?"

Pete snickered. "I kissed a girl, and I liked it? Yeah, it was fine. I imagined they were guys, but they didn't know that."

"No wonder you got to be such a good kisser. You had lots of practice."

"Yup."

"Was Luke the first guy you kissed?"

"Yes." His expression said, *And no more will be said about that.* "I'm sorry I'm not as good at sex as I am at kissing."

"Pete. You're *great* at sex. There are just certain things you don't do. What you do, though, you do *very* well."

"Hm. I want to show you something I've been thinking about." He took a pen and pad of paper out of the storage compartment in the ottoman. "I showed this to my therapist today, and she said it could be helpful." He drew a line across the middle of the page. "Think about sex as a sliding scale." He put an X on one side of the line. "Here's where we are now, and here…" He put an X on the other end of the line. "…is your ideal, with complete equality in fucking." He indicated the area between the X's. "There's space in here. If you and I could agree on what goes in that space, in what order, maybe that would help."

"Hm. Okay. What do you think is in that space?"

"Well…" He scrubbed his face with one hand. "The first thing I thought of is blowjobs."

That surprised me. "Really? We do that."

"I know. But – I could do more. I'm not as good at it as you are. You've had more experience. While I was sucking face with girls in college, you were sucking dick with the spoiled cowardly Giants fan."

I laughed. "Have I ever complained?"

"No. But I know I could improve my technique. And there are no psychological barriers there. You don't mind if I get more practice, do you?"

"Are you kidding? Practice all you want. You can start tonight."

He grinned. "Okay."

"Just out of curiosity, what else is on this sliding scale?"

He tensed a little. "This one is harder – but I'd like to work on being able to hug you from behind."

That seemed like a tiny step to me, but as Alex had pointed out, it wasn't up to me. "I'd like that. Especially in bed. Do you know what spooning is?"

"Um – on our sides, back to front?"

"Yeah. It's always been a really comfortable way for me to sleep. And since it's lying down, on our sides – that should be less of a psychological barrier than standing, right?"

"Yeah. It should be. So – that can be a long-term goal."

"Absolutely." I took the paper and pen out of his hands and set them aside. "Now, about that blowjob…"

Friday, March 29

I drove my VW to work Friday morning, Pete riding shotgun. He was doing some preliminary research for a paper on psychopathology in community college students and brought his laptop. We made a point of holding hands while walking toward the circulation desk. Connie and Grace were both there – Connie with a smirk on her face, Grace with a look of horror. I said, "Connie, you remember my boyfriend Pete, right?"

"Right. We met back in the fall." Connie grinned at us. "Are you here working today?"

Pete grinned back. "Yeah, I have some research to do. Jamie's going to set me up in the Reading Room. Good to see you again." None of us looked at Grace.

I got Pete settled in the Reading Room. He'd been here before, but we were performing for Grace this time. I'd gotten him a guest logon ID for the wireless system, and I made sure he got connected before I left.

"If you need any articles, email me."

"I will." Pete winked at me. "See you at lunch."

I went to my office and got to work. A handful of the students in my class had turned in their first assignment, and I graded those and answered questions on the discussion board. I had some book and article requests from faculty to hunt down, and Pete emailed me three times for articles.

At lunchtime, we collected Liz and ate outside at the North Campus Student Center. Liz and I talked about our librarian-law enforcement paper, and Pete gave his opinions. The rest of the day passed uneventfully. Clinton hadn't learned anything about Terry Moynihan yet, but he was going to talk to a couple of people he knew over the weekend that might be able to help.

At 5:00 I closed up shop, and Pete and I drove the short distance to Kevin and Abby's. Kevin wasn't home yet, but I let us in with the guest pass and a spare key that he'd given me. I got two beers out of the fridge, and we made ourselves comfortable. Pete said, "Which sister of Abby's had the twins?"

"The next youngest one. Amy." Abby was the middle of five girls, all with A names. All five lived in LA; Amy was up in the Valley somewhere.

"How old are they?"

"Not very – a couple of weeks. I guess the girls are taking turns helping out."

"Is Abby coming with us tomorrow night?"

"Yeah. She'll be back by then." Ali was taking us all out tomorrow evening to repay us for helping her remove sod last weekend.

We were on our second beer by the time Kevin got home. He closed the door and clapped his hands twice. "On your feet. Change of plans."

We grumbled and stayed where we were.

"Come on. There's no baseball on TV tonight, but the Dodgers are playing the Angels at Dodger Stadium. Next to last game of spring training. We can eat there."

I waved my beer bottle at him. "You have to drive."

"Deal."

We arrived just in time for the first pitch and got cheap seats near the top of the stadium with almost no one else around us. Pete took our orders and went to the concession stand, and I grabbed the opportunity to question Kevin. "Tell me about Luke."

Kevin frowned. "What about him?"

"Anything about him. All I know is that Pete didn't trust him, and he didn't have any complaints about Pete's approach to sex. Every time I mention his name, Pete clams up."

"Should I start from the beginning?"

"Please."

"Luke is an IT guy. At the time he worked for the company that had the city contract. He and Pete met when Luke came to put new computers in the squad cars."

"An *IT* guy?"

"Yeah, so?"

"If you remember, I had some problems with an IT guy last year. Plus... Pete with a computer geek?"

"Hard to picture, isn't it? Anyway, Luke picked up on – something – from Pete, and flirted with him the whole time he was there. Pete wasn't out in the department then, and didn't do anything to encourage him. But I guess Luke slipped him his phone number, and they started seeing each other."

"How long was this before I moved here?"

"Um..." Kevin thought for a moment. "Not quite three years, I guess. They dated for almost two years and Pete was keeping it quiet with no trouble – but then Luke outed him to the department."

"*What??*"

"Yep. He called HR and asked what benefits would be available to same-sex partners, and told them he was Pete's boyfriend. HR called Pete about it, and the word was out."

"That *asshole*."

"I know. Pete should have dumped his sorry ass right then, but Luke wet himself apologizing, said he didn't think, blah blah blah. Of course he'd planned it all out, thinking it would get Pete to let him move in with Pete and Uncle Arthur. That was never gonna happen; Uncle Arthur couldn't stand Luke."

"But Pete didn't dump him."

"No. But that was the beginning of the end, although the end took a long time to come. Other cops were starting to give Pete grief about being gay, and Pete rightly blamed Luke for that. Pete had finished his master's level classes, and Luke was bugging him to apply to Ph.D. programs up in the Bay area because Luke wanted to work at Google. Pete didn't want to move and didn't apply to any schools up there, so that pissed Luke off. And then you moved here."

"Pete told me once that he'd fallen for me as soon as he met me."

"He did."

"But it took him almost another year to break up with Luke."

"It did. You started seeing Dan almost immediately, then Nick. And Pete didn't have any experience breaking up with anyone. I think he didn't know how to go about it with Luke."

"He figured it out eventually."

"Yeah, but the two of you weren't in the right place for each other that first time. And Luke started begging Pete to take him back almost as soon as they'd broken up."

"I didn't know *that*. I thought it wasn't for several months."

"It was only about a month."

"Jeez. So he just wore Pete down."

"Probably. And Uncle Arthur had just died – Pete might have been looking for comfort in familiarity at that point."

"Didn't he know he'd wreck his friendship with you?"

Kevin shrugged. "I don't know if he thought about that. It couldn't have surprised him too much, though."

"What does Luke look like?"

"He's about six feet, skinny. His coloring's similar to yours."

I made a face. Kevin laughed. "Hey, I know that Abby and my ex resemble each other. Some guys have types." He nudged my knee with his. "Is this helping you?"

"Yeah. I needed to know all of that. And I don't think Pete would ever have told me."

"He might have, but not all at once."

"Yeah, he does that, kind of doles out information in bits and pieces. We're working on that, though."

"It's a cop thing. You get used to not giving too much away at once."

"You don't do it."

"I don't do it with you. Or Abby, or the rest of the family. I'm better at separating my professional life from my personal life than Pete ever was."

"He said there were several reasons he left the police force. I guess that was one of them."

"Yep."

Pete came back and distributed food and drink. "What did I miss?"

We both said "Nothing" at the same time. Pete gave us a funny look, but Kevin started talking about the Dodgers' chances this year, and Pete was quickly distracted. The fact that he was mildly buzzed probably helped.

The game was a good one for those who enjoy lots of runs – the Dodgers won 9 to 8. With all that scoring the game finished late. Pete and I had drunk a couple more beers apiece and weren't in shape to drive, so we had a debate about whether Kevin would take us home or we'd spend the night at his place. We ended up staying the night. Kevin found pajama bottoms and t-shirts for both of us and inflated the full-sized air mattress that he and Abby kept for guests. He tossed a quilt over the mattress, and Pete and I crashed.

Saturday, March 30

I woke up the next morning on the floor. Pete was sprawled across the entire air mattress; one of his arms was flung across my forehead. How did I sleep through that? Not to mention rolling off the mattress? My mouth felt like an army of Labrador retrievers had marched through it, shedding their undercoats as they went. And I had no toothbrush.

I slithered out from under Pete's arm and got to my feet. There was no sign of Kevin. I went in the bathroom, found Kevin's toothpaste, put some on my finger, and rubbed it around my mouth, concentrating on my tongue. I found a clean towel in the tiny linen closet and went back in the living room to retrieve my clothes, then took a shower. I had just turned the water off when Kevin stuck his head in. "I'll give you a t-shirt and sweats to wear home so you don't have to put yesterday's clothes on."

"Thanks, but I need underwear and socks too."

"Socks I can do. Underwear – can't you go commando from here to your house?"

"In sweatpants? Only if someone walks in front of me."

He laughed and disappeared. I was drying my hair when he opened the door again and tossed in a pair of socks and an unopened three-pack of boxer briefs. "Early birthday present." They were a size bigger than my usual, but they'd get me home without embarrassment, and they'd fit Pete.

By the time Pete showered and we got home it was 10:15. Kevin had fed us cereal, and we'd both taken some of his aspirin. I went to the fridge and got Cokes for both of us. Pete said, "I'm going to call Mark Jones's mom. If she's going to be home, do you want to ride out there tomorrow?"

"Sure. But we'll have to lay off the booze tonight if we're going out there and back tomorrow."

"I'll have to lay off the booze tonight anyway because of how much I drank last night." Pete drained his first Coke and got a second one. "And we don't have any exercise planned for today."

"So, we deserve one weekend off. If it'll make you feel better, why don't we go join the Y today?"

So that's what we did. Pete talked to Mark's mom, who said she'd love to see us tomorrow. I did laundry and cleaned the bathrooms while Pete ran the vacuum cleaner. We drove down to the Y and joined – they made us each buy an individual membership – then came home and took a nap.

At 7:00, Mel and Ali came to pick us up. Kevin and Abby were already with them, in Ali's van. We went to a jazz club in Venice called El Caribe. It was technically a gay bar; I'd been here several times in the past with Scott. It was straight-friendly, though, so Kevin and Abby wouldn't feel out of place. It was a nice place, with Key West-style décor and good-looking bartenders. And they didn't water down their drinks.

Tonight there was a trio playing. They were pretty good. Ali was paying for the drinks, but Pete stuck to ginger ale. I ordered a Long Island iced tea and nursed it. Kevin was able to drink this evening, since Ali was driving, and he, Mel and Abby kept the bartender hopping.

I asked Abby, "How are the twins?"

"They're fine. It's their two-year-old hellspawn brother that I was assigned to. The kid's jealous of the babies and he's being a real shit."

We all commiserated and renewed our vows of childlessness.

We called it a night fairly early and were home and in bed by 11:00. I was falling asleep when Pete asked, "Did you ever think about getting married?"

Whoa. I snapped to attention. "Um – no. I always knew that wasn't going to be a possibility for me."

"But now it will be, most likely. The Supreme Court is going to rule on DOMA and Prop 8 in June."

"Yeah. But the answer to your question is no. I still haven't thought about it. Have you?"

He said softly, "Yeah. I have." He didn't elaborate.

Oh shit. We lay there in silence for a minute. I didn't know what to say. The truth was I hadn't considered it for a minute. Of course I hoped that the court ruled in favor of marriage equality. Ali and Mel had gotten married here in California back in the short window of opportunity in 2008 that had closed with the passage of Prop 8. Mel's law partner - my dad's buddy Neil - and his husband, Mark, had also married then. I'd gone to both weddings, and I'd be delighted if both couples could finally qualify for federal marriage benefits.

But I'd never thought it was for me.

Pete and I had been together for nine months. We'd begun living together just a few days after we'd begun dating again because of the fire in my apartment. A week later, Pete had been shot in the shoulder, and I'd been hospitalized after a severe asthma attack. Things had gotten intense very quickly for us. We'd had a honeymoon phase for the first six months until Pete had told me about his abuse, and since then we'd been struggling. I had every intention of working this relationship out. Pete was a jewel, and I'd be an idiot to give him up.

But – marriage? He couldn't be thinking about us getting married – could he?

And if he was – what would I do about it?

All of these thoughts were zooming around in my head, and I still hadn't thought of anything to say. It felt to me like Pete was a little tense, but other than that, I had no idea what he was thinking. I was about to ask when he said, "Good night, Jamie," and rolled away from me.

I whispered, "Good night." I figured I'd screwed up – but I didn't know what to do about it.

I couldn't make my brain stop working, and I couldn't get comfortable in bed. I tried rolling to my side, then to my back, then to my side again, but sleep eluded me. Finally, I got out of bed so that all my thrashing around wouldn't wake Pete. I quietly opened the door that led from our bedroom to a small balcony-style deck and slipped outside. I sat down in one of the two Adirondack chairs that were there, leaned back and closed my eyes.

Thinking was getting me nowhere, so I tried not to think. I listened to the sounds of Santa Monica at night – traffic from Wilshire, a cat yowling somewhere, an occasional shout, distant sirens. I could keep myself from thinking, but I couldn't stop feeling. And I felt terrible.

Pete and I had gotten along great for six months. Then he'd told me his big secret, and I'd reacted badly. And now Pete's mention of marriage had caught me completely off guard. He couldn't possibly be thinking about getting married yet. Could he? And if he was, what would I say?

I knew I wasn't ready to get married. Hell, I'd never even considered it in my wildest dreams. If he asked now, I'd have to tell him no. What would that do to our relationship?

And – if I dug even deeper into my psyche – this brought up the issue of sexual incompatibility again. Marriage was a whole 'nother level of commitment. Could I promise that Pete would be enough for me for the rest of my life? Deep down, I was afraid that I couldn't.

I'd opened my eyes at some point, and I closed them again, trying to hold back the tears. But it didn't work. They leaked out anyway.

I awoke to shaking. Were we having an earthquake? And where the hell was I? I struggled up through layers of consciousness. No, no earthquake - I was shaking because I was shivering, cold down to my bones.

And because Pete was shaking my shoulder. "Jamie, c'mon, wake up..."

I opened my eyes. It was dark. Why was I outside? Oh, yeah, because I couldn't sleep. It looked like I'd solved that problem, except now I was drenched with condensation, and freezing.

"What the hell are you doing out here?" Pete held his hand out to me.

I took it and let him pull me up. "I couldn't sleep, and I didn't want to wake you up. So I came out here to relax."

"Looks like you accomplished that okay." He tugged at my hand. "C'mon. Let's get you in the shower. We have to get you warmed up."

I let him lead me inside, into the bathroom. I peeled off my damp pajamas while Pete got the shower going and took off his own pajamas. The shower was soon producing billowing clouds of steam. Pete flipped on the exhaust fan and pulled me into the shower with him. He guided me backwards so that the water was hitting my shoulders and upper back. It felt wonderful. Pete wrapped his arms around me and held me while the shivering lessened. I held on to him for dear life. Finally, I started to feel a little warmer. Pete turned me around, so the water was now hitting my chest, and wrapped his arms around me again.

My brain finally kicked into gear enough to ask, "What time is it?"

"It's about 3:30. Something woke me up, I think a noise from outside, and I didn't know where you were. Then I saw the door cracked. Why'd you go outside and not to the office or downstairs?"

"I didn't want to think. I thought maybe if I just listened to the night sounds for a while, I could come back to bed and sleep. I guess it worked too well."

The water was starting to cool, so Pete turned it off. I immediately started to feel chilled again. He pulled a stack of towels out from under the sink and started rubbing me down. "Still not completely warm?"

"No. But that's helping."

"Good." He switched towels, then handed the dry towel to me. "Here, dry your hair. I'll grab some sweats for you." He disappeared into the bedroom then came back with sweatpants and a t-shirt. I stopped to put them on then kept rubbing my hair dry. Pete put his own pajamas back on, and hung up the wet towels and my wet pajamas. I rubbed my hair a little more then climbed back into bed. Pete pulled the covers up over us. "Better?"

"Yeah." I'd finally quit shivering, and was starting to feel normal again. We lay there for a minute, getting comfortable, then something occurred to me. "Hey."

"Hm?"

"Do you realize what you did in the shower?"

"What?"

"You were holding me from behind, standing up. You didn't even think about it."

"Seemed like the thing to do at the time." I could hear the smile in his voice.

"Yep. Just keep that thought." And it was on that thought that I was able to go back to sleep.

Sunday, March 31

It seemed like one minute later that the alarm went off, but it was 8:00, much later than I usually got up. Pete was already up; I could smell toasted bagels. We ate quickly and were on the road by 8:30 for the two-hour trip. Pete maneuvered through the freeways expertly, and by 9:30 we were on the 15 headed north.

We hadn't said anything about last night yet. Once he had the cruise control set, Pete said, "I'm sorry I brought up marriage last night."

"You don't have to apologize for bringing it up. You just caught me off guard."

"I realize that now. Spending the evening with Ali and Mel – it made me think about it."

"You've thought about it before."

"Yeah, but mostly in abstract form. Would I want to get married someday, given the right person and the laws changing? I always thought I would."

"I truly have never considered it for myself. I'm not against it, I just – it never occurred to me."

"You seemed kind of freaked out last night when I brought it up."

"Not freaked out, exactly, just – it was unexpected. I'm not – I don't think we've been together long enough to be considering marriage yet."

"Right." That didn't seem to be the answer he wanted.

"Do you think we should consider it?"

"I agree, we haven't been together long enough to get married. But when we have been together long enough, when we've worked out all this – stuff – would I like to be married to you? Yeah."

"Okay."

"You're not ruling it out."

"No, I'm not ruling it out."

"Good."

I was going to have to work on my commitment issues, though. Maybe Dr. Bibbins had discharged me too early. Speaking of which – "Do you remember what you did last night?"

"Hugging you from behind in the shower? Yeah."

"What were you thinking when you were doing it?"

"I wasn't thinking about what I was doing. I just wanted to get you warmed up as quickly as possible."

"So it didn't feel wrong to you."

"No. It felt right at the time."

"I think that's a very good sign."

"A sign of what?"

"That you might be ready to work on spooning."

"That's really important to you."

"It is. I love to sleep that way. I love being held that way. I've missed doing that."

He nodded. "It *shouldn't* be a problem. It's not – there's no bad memory associated with lying down."

"Can I ask you something about that?"

His expression was guarded, but he said, "Yeah."

"Was it always standing?"

"Yes." Period. That was fine; that's all I'd wanted to know. There was something else about spooning – that position was one that, in my experience, often led to fucking. If Pete could lie with me in that position, maybe he could fuck me in that position. That would be a big step – but maybe not impossible.

A tiny little flicker of hope ignited in my brain.

We drove out of the mountains into the desert. It always amazed me to see how empty it was out here. We passed the exit for Victorville, where Pete's grandparents had lived, and didn't pass another sign of civilization until we got to Barstow.

We left the 15 and let it continue on its merry way to Vegas. We took Barstow Road north to East Mountain View Street. When we turned onto Mountain View, Pete pointed to the left. "The church."

There it was. A perfectly ordinary looking church. I took a deep breath and blew it out. Pete didn't say anything more.

We continued on into a residential neighborhood with streets named for women. Pete turned onto one of them, and almost immediately into a driveway. "This is the Jones's house. The Smith's, now, I guess."

It was a trim little blue house with a few patches of green and a towering palm tree in the front yard. The front door opened as we got out of the car, and Mrs. Smith met us halfway. She wrapped Pete up in a hug, then took my hand and gave it a squeeze. "I'm so glad to see you two. Come on in."

Mrs. Smith led the way into her living room, an airy space with light woods and cream-colored fabrics, with throws and blankets adding splashes of color. "You boys have a seat. Would you like some iced tea?"

We said yes and made ourselves comfortable. Mrs. Smith returned quickly with three glasses of tea and a plate of cookies on a tray. I took an oatmeal cookie – still warm – and took a bite. It was heavenly. I made appreciative sounds and Mrs. Smith smiled. "These were Pete's favorite when he was little. I hope they still are."

Pete smiled. "Oh, they are."

We chatted for a few minutes then Pete asked, "How are you doing?"

Mrs. Smith sighed. "It still doesn't seem real. I keep expecting him to call, you know? But poor Hunter. He's having a terrible time."

Hunter was Mark's boyfriend. Pete asked, "Did he come stay with you, like you wanted?"

"No. He's staying with his brother. He can't bring himself to go back into the apartment, and I can't blame him."

"He'll have to go back, at some point."

"Yes. And it will have to be soon. He can't afford the rent on the place himself. Mark made a lot more money than he did, and Mark paid most of the rent."

I asked, "What does Hunter do?"

"He's a wardrobe assistant at CBS. He loves his job, but he doesn't make a lot of money."

Pete said, "I was talking to Steve a couple of nights ago, and he reminded me that Mark had taken a year off between high school and college. What did he do that year?"

Mrs. Smith frowned. "Mostly, he drank. He said he didn't want to go to college. He got a job answering phones at one of the insurance offices in town – the broker was a friend of Mark's father. I told him that he couldn't live here if he was going to be drunk all the time, so he was living with his dad, whose second marriage was breaking up. It was a bad time. But thank God that Barry, his employer, took an interest in Mark. He got him to stop drinking and convinced him to go to college. Mark had gotten interested in the insurance business, and he'd always been good at math, so he decided to be an actuary. From then on he didn't have any problems that I knew about. At least not with substance abuse."

"But he had other problems?"

Mrs. Smith sighed. "I understand this happens sometimes when young men come out for the first time. Mark went a little wild in college from a sexual standpoint. He was with a different boy every weekend. I only heard about this from his stepsister. I tried to talk to him about it, but he'd say, 'Oh, Mom, I'm just having fun,' and change the subject. But he eventually settled down, so I didn't think it caused him any permanent harm."

I asked, "He had other long-term boyfriends before Hunter?"

"Yes. He was about 25 when he met Jim. They met at a bar, but Jim was a nice boy. It was the first long-term relationship for either of them. They were happy for about ten years, then something happened – I don't know what. When I asked Mark, he said they had 'grown apart,' whatever that means, but I always thought there was more to it."

"But then he met Hunter."

"Yes, and they seemed perfectly happy." Mrs. Smith gazed out the front window into the distance. "I don't know why he – I just don't…" She trailed off. We sat quietly for a minute, then Mrs. Smith gathered her composure. "So, Pete. Tell me about your career."

He did. She asked about my work, and I answered her questions. She and Pete talked about some of the other kids Pete had known growing up. We ate more cookies. At about noon, Mr. Smith came home, and we chatted with him while Mrs. Smith put a pan of lasagna in the oven and assembled a salad. We ate lunch; the lasagna was delicious and I had two helpings. After lunch Mr. Smith cleaned up the kitchen, refusing all help from us. Mrs. Smith grinned as she led us back into the living room. "See why I keep him around?"

We stayed a little longer, but started saying our goodbyes around 2:00. As we were leaving, I asked Mrs. Smith, "Do you remember Jim's last name? Mark's former boyfriend?"

"Of course. It was Lengyel." She spelled it for me.

"Do you know what happened to him?"

"No, I'm sorry to say I lost touch. He wasn't a local boy, and he might have moved back to – where was it, Wendell?"

"San Diego, down that way. Carlsbad, I want to say."

Carlsbad was the next town south of Oceanside. Maybe I could find something out about Jim Lengyel.

Pete said, "Jamie and I have been trying to figure out what happened to Mark, that he would do this."

Mrs. Smith said, "So have we. But if you can find anything new, please let me know."

I asked, "Do you think Hunter would be willing to talk to us?"

"I'm sure he would. I'll call him and ask him to get in touch with you."

Monday, April 1

I drove to work, since my class met tonight. I was fixing a broken link on the class website when Clinton came to my door. "Good morning, Dr. Brodie. I hope I am not interrupting your work."

"Not at all. Have a seat."

"I spoke with two people over the weekend who knew of Father Terry Moynihan. I have some information for you."

"Clinton, that's awesome." I grabbed a pen and sticky note out of my desk. "Shoot."

"Father Moynihan came to Barstow from a parish in Santa Barbara. There had been complaints there that he was spending too much time with the young people and not enough on his other duties. His transfer to Barstow was seen as sufficient punishment, apparently. He was in Barstow for six years, at which time he was transferred again, to a parish in Imperial County."

Imperial County was east of San Diego, desert with a stretch of irrigated agricultural land down the center. Its biggest town was El Centro, which would have been a lateral move from Barstow for Father Terry in terms of size and culture. "Was there a reason given for his second transfer?"

"Yes. There was an accusation of sexual abuse from the father of an altar boy."

"But that didn't appear in documentation anywhere."

"No."

"What happened to him after that?"

"Four years later, he was transferred again, to Bishop." Another remote assignment. "No reason was given. Six years after that, he resigned from the priesthood. The official reason was that he wanted to pursue another career path. The unofficial reason was that he had once again been accused of sexual abuse of an altar boy."

A serial offender. And the church had just kept moving him around, like they had so many others. "Any idea where he is now?"

"My friends did not know. But they are trying to find out."
Clinton gave me a look. "May I assume that you think Pete's friend
may have been a victim of Father Moynihan's?"

"We know he was. Mark – Pete's friend – had told Pete's
brother about it, years ago."

"Ah. But he was not part of the recent lawsuits and
settlement."

"No. He'd never told anyone in his family about the abuse.
They still don't know."

Clinton nodded. "The troubles within the church continue to
be in the news, of course. And our new Holy Father does not have a
history of punishing pedophile priests."

"No? I don't know anything about him."

"No." Clinton didn't elaborate. He was scowling. I'd never
seen him do that before.

"It's hard to imagine, though, that general news about
abusive priests, or even the election of the pope, would be enough to
trigger a suicide."

"I agree. It is more likely, in my opinion, to be something
personal." Clinton stood and bowed. "I will leave you to your work."

"Thanks, Clinton. I really appreciate this."

I thought about what he'd said. Clinton had confirmed our
suspicions about Father Terry, but I didn't see how this information
could be related to Mark's suicide. The abuse had to be a huge chunk
of the fabric of Mark's life, as it was for Pete. But it had been over
twenty years. There had to be something more specific, more recent.

We needed to talk to Mark's boyfriend. In the meantime,
maybe his old boyfriend could shed some light on the subject. I had
a friend in Carlsbad, a kid who'd played youth rugby with me,
named Damon Peña. He had older siblings who would be about the
same age as Mark and Jim. Maybe he'd know something. I found his
number in my phone and sent him a text. *Hey, got a question for
you. Call when you can.*

I was eating lunch when Damon called back. "Jamie, hey! What's up?"

We hadn't talked for a couple of months, so we briefly caught each other up on work and family stuff. Then I asked, "Do you know a guy from Carlsbad named Jim Lengyel? Probably a few years older than us."

"Um – the name sounds familiar. Why?"

I gave a very brief explanation of why we wanted to talk to Jim. Damon said, "I don't know if he lives in Carlsbad or not, but my sisters probably would. Let me talk to them this evening and I'll get back to you."

The rest of the day flew by. Grace walked past the reference desk three times while Liz and I were there, but we were too busy to even mention it. At 5:00, I went outside to meet Pete, who'd brought me dinner – shrimp pasta salad. We sat on the steps of the library and ate, and I told him about my conversations with Clinton and Damon. We didn't have much time to talk about it, though, since my class started at 5:30. We were seen by Grace, who passed by on her way out of the building. She glared at Pete and kept going.

My class flew by. I had 17 students, and the one who'd called me last week was apparently the only needy one. The rest asked intelligent questions and seemed to be enthusiastic about the subject. At 7:30 I put them to work on an in-class assignment for 45 minutes and checked my phone. Damon had left a voice mail. "Jim Lengyel lives in LA now. He's on faculty at USC, in the occupational therapy department."

That was enough information to find Jim. Now I had to decide how to approach him.

It was nearly 10:00 when I got home, and I didn't want to think about Mark Jones any more this evening. Pete had the lights down and the music low. We cuddled for a while, talking about our days, then Pete said, "Ready for your question?"

"Sure, go ahead."

"Have you ever considered suicide?"

Ugh. It seemed we were going to talk about Mark after all. "No. Never."

"Not even when Ethan broke up with you?"

"No. I was heartbroken, sure, but I had a degree to finish, and that helped me to keep putting one foot in front of the other. Of course it also helped that my dad and Jeff spent a fortune in phone calls talking me through it."

"Heh. Not Kevin?"

"No. Kevin and Jennifer were in their downward spiral then. He had his own problems."

"Ah. Yeah, that's right. That was happening at the same time."

"Mm hm." I pulled away a little so I could look at Pete's face. "Have *you* ever considered it?"

He took a moment to answer. "There were times when I was younger that I wished I could just disappear. But I never had a plan to make that happen."

"I'm so glad. What if I'd never met you? I'd be homeless."

Pete huffed a soft laugh. "I'm sure you'd have figured something out."

Since we were sort of on the subject – "Can I ask you something else?"

"Two for the price of one, huh? I guess so."

I looked Pete in the face again. "If I find Terry Moynihan, what are you going to do about it?"

His expression grew hard. His cop face. "I haven't decided yet."

"Pete, you can't confront him."

"Why not?"

"Because you could be arrested. If he's a private citizen now, you can't harass him. You know the law better than I do."

He was quiet for a moment. "We'll see." He didn't say anything else.

I sighed inwardly. "I sure know how to spoil a mood, don't I?"

Pete laughed a little, and I felt him relax. "Nah. I'm the one who did that, with the suicide talk. So I've got another question for you."

"What's that?"

"How am I doing with the blow jobs?"

"You know, it's been a couple of days – I don't remember. You're going to have to remind me."

Tuesday, April 2

The first thing I did at work the next morning was find Jim Lengyel on USC's website. I sent him a carefully worded email, briefly introducing myself and my connection to Mark Jones, and telling him why I'd like to talk to him. I clicked send, thinking I might not hear from the guy.

I had to give a presentation to a class on mythology, which was not my strong suit, so I spent the rest of the morning preparing for that. We were busy at reference again. When Clinton arrived, he had to wait to speak to us. Finally he was able to approach the desk. I said, "Hi, Clinton."

He said, "The word of the day is *cark*." He bowed and turned away.

Liz looked the word up. "It means care or worry."

"Hm. Clinton's concerned about me trying to find this priest."

"Does he need to be?"

"No." But I wasn't so sure about that.

When I got back to my office, I was surprised to find an email from Jim Lengyel. He was willing to talk to me, if I would call after 5:00. I emailed back quickly to say I would do that, then texted Pete to let him know I'd be late getting home. He texted back to say he'd come pick me up. Good – another opportunity for Grace to see us in action.

At 5:00, Pete came to my door. I asked, "Did Grace see you?"

"I made sure she did. I stood there and talked to Connie for about ten minutes, all about you and me. Grace was in the back at first, but then she came out and saw me. She was pretending not to listen, but her face was getting redder and redder."

"Ha. Good." I pulled up the email with Jim's number and dialed.

When he answered, I said, "Jim, this is Jamie Brodie. Thank you for talking to me."

"No problem. I talked to Damon Peña and he said you were okay." Jim's voice was high-pitched almost to the point of being squeaky. "I'm glad to talk to someone about Mark. I didn't want to bother his family because I knew Mark's new boyfriend would be with them."

"You didn't go to the funeral."

"No. I couldn't."

"Mark's mother said you all were together for ten years."

"Almost eleven, actually. It killed me to leave him. I thought we'd be together forever."

"Mark's mom said that Mark told her you all grew apart."

Jim snorted. "Yeah, that sounds like what he would have told her. It's not what happened, though."

"What did happen?"

"We started having serious money issues. Mark was making investments with his money that I didn't agree with, and he wanted to put our money into it too."

"What kind of investments?"

"Hedge funds. The risky stuff. When the economy tanked, he lost a bundle. He'd started earning it back, but hadn't gotten anywhere near recovering it all. Then he started wanting to invest our money too."

"You had a joint account."

"Yeah. We each put an equal amount into a joint account, and that's what we used for paying the bills and also for things like saving for vacations. We both had our own money too, but I had a lot less left over after I contributed my half. Mark always made a lot more money than I did. I didn't care what he did with his own money, but I didn't want any of ours to be at risk."

"So you argued about that."

"We did. He was really insistent. And then – after I'd said no over and over – he went ahead and did it anyway."

"Oh my God."

"Yeah. And the particular fund he was in was apparently very poorly managed, and he lost a lot of our money. I had to dig into my own savings to cover our utility bills that last month. So I left him. I couldn't trust him anymore."

"But this was a couple of years ago, right?"

"Yeah. I know what you're thinking – what could that have had to do with his suicide? And the answer is, I don't know. Unless he was still making bad investments."

"You hadn't had any contact with him since you split?"

"No. I packed up what I could in my car and drove away, and didn't look back. I've rebuilt my life."

"Was he day trading?"

"To some extent, yeah, but you can't do that with hedge funds. You have to go through a fund manager. He had a guy down in La Jolla. I don't remember his name."

"You didn't keep any records that would have had that information?"

"No. When I left I only took what was mine. I left Mark to clean up the mess - if he even did. He may have kept right on doing what he was doing."

"Were you surprised when you heard what had happened?"

"To some extent. But when Mark lost all that money he changed. It was like – a gambling addict, I guess. He was desperate to make the money back and he was thinking about it all the time."

"It seems weird to me for an actuary to involve himself in that kind of risky trading. Who would know better the dangers?"

"That's what I thought too. I even talked to him about that at the time, or tried to. But he basically blew me off with the 'I'm a professional and I know what I'm doing and you don't' attitude."

"I'm sorry."

"Yeah, me too. He was a great guy, really. We had a terrific life before he got involved with this fund manager."

"Had you ever known him to be depressed?"

"Not clinically, no. He'd get angry when the stock market wasn't doing what he wanted it to, but he was never sad or depressed about anything. He didn't even seem that sad to see me go."

"Did he drink?"

"No. Not at all. He was really against it. He knew exactly how many years it cut off the average male's life span."

Interesting. Mark had been legally intoxicated when he died. Somewhere along the line, he'd lost his aversion to drink. I wondered if Mark had ever told Jim about his abuse, but I couldn't just come out and ask that. "Can you think of anything else that might have contributed to Mark's death? Anything in his past?"

"No. I mean, his parents were divorced, but whose weren't? I've thought about it, and I really can't come up with any reason that he'd do this. Unless he'd had more financial problems."

So Mark hadn't told Jim. Or maybe Jim was holding back. Either way, it sounded like Mark's financial status was a possible trigger. "Jim, thank you so much for talking to me. I appreciate it a lot. If you do think of anything else, would you mind sending me an email?"

"No problem." We said goodbye and I hung up.

Pete said, "So Mark had financial problems."

"Maybe." I told Pete what Jim had said. "If he was still losing money, it could have contributed to his mental status."

"But we don't know if he was."

"No." I sighed. "We still have to talk to his boyfriend."

"Yeah. But right now I'm hungry."

We went to 800 Degrees for pizza then went home. We both had work to do. I spent the evening answering email and discussion board questions from my students and grading the work they'd done in class last night, and Pete was grading papers. When we finally got to bed, Pete put his head on my shoulder. "Thank you for working so hard on this thing with Mark."

"You're welcome. I'm curious too. What could make a guy like him kill himself? But it might have been money problems."

"Maybe. But I still think it has to have something to do with Terry Moynihan."

"Clinton's still looking for him."

"Good." Pete reached for my hand and laced his fingers with mine. "What's your question tonight?"

"What was your favorite book when you were a kid?"

"You'll laugh."

"No, I won't."

"Okay – it was the Hardy Boys books."

"Hey, lots of kids loved the Hardy Boys. Why would I laugh at that?"

"Well, they're pretty cheesy, aren't they?"

"For adults, yeah, but for kids they're great. Anything that gets boys to read is a good thing. That was the best thing about the Harry Potter books. They got so many kids to read that might not have otherwise."

"Yeah. But the Hardy Boys were hardly consistent with proper law enforcement procedure."

I laughed. "Well, no. Neither was Miss Marple, but Agatha Christie got away with it."

"Did you read the Hardy Boys?"

"Of course. All three of us did. But they weren't my favorite."

"What was yours?"

"Watership Down."

"I never read that."

"Really? I'll have to see if Dad's still got my copy. Everyone should read that."

"Okay, I will. Did that count as my question?"

"Not if you've got another one you want to ask."

"I do. I know you told me you first had anal sex with Ethan. But what was your very first sexual experience?"

"Oh, wow. I was thirteen. My best friend Robbie and I were wrestling over the TV remote in his room, and we sort of ended up in a tangled heap, groin to groin, and we both got hard. So we jerked each other off."

"Was Robbie gay?"

"Gay or bi, I'm not sure which. But he'd never admit to being anything but straight. He had a girlfriend in high school, but he didn't sleep with her. He slept with me."

"Maybe he was straight, and just experimenting."

"Maybe, but I don't think so. He liked sucking dick waaaaay too much to be straight."

Pete laughed. "Where is he now?"

"No idea. He went to the Naval Academy. I heard he got kicked out but since then I don't know."

"Kicked out for being gay? Or getting caught with a guy?"

"I'm not sure. I heard it was for drinking. Knowing Robbie it was probably on purpose."

"Sounds like a troubled youth."

"Mm hm." I was getting sleepy. "Say goodnight, Gracie."

Pete snickered. "You sure you want to call me that?"

"Oh God no! Argh!"

Wednesday, April 3

Connie stopped by my office the next morning to inform me that Grace had complained that I was flaunting my boyfriend.

"Complained to who?"

"James." James Wygant, our access services director.

"What did he say?"

"He just laughed and told her to grow up. So now she's pouting."

"Good. Maybe she will grow up."

"I think she's regrouping."

"Oh, God. Please, Connie, make her stop."

Connie laughed. "I'm trying."

"I'm serious. When she turns into a crazy stalker and shows up at my house, I'm telling the cops it was your fault."

She went away laughing.

At reference, Clinton stopped to talk rather than give us a word for the day. "I have more information about Terry Moynihan."

He seemed hesitant – something I'd never observed in Clinton. I said, "You're not sure if you should tell me."

"It is unclear to me where this inquiry will lead."

"It's unclear to me too, Clinton."

He nodded. "I appreciate your honesty."

"Do you have an exact location?"

"No. My friends were unable to ascertain that. However, they did learn that he is still in California and is living under his own name."

"But that's all they could find out?"

"Yes. Most of the people who knew of Moynihan have retired or died. All that remains is rumor. What I have given you are the rumors that are consistent. Other than that, there are no two reports that match."

I sighed. "Okay. Thank you, Clinton. I truly appreciate what you've done."

He stood, bowed and walked away. Liz asked, "Why do you want to find this guy so badly?"

"Pete's convinced that he had something to do with his friend's suicide."

"How is that possible, if no one even knows where he is?"

I didn't have an answer.

I was back in my office when Pete called. "I got a call from Hunter Mitchell today. He wants to talk to us."

Mark's boyfriend. "Hey, that's great. When?"

"He wants to meet tomorrow evening. He said he'd come to the house and I invited him to dinner."

"Oh, okay. That was nice."

"Yeah, well, I figured he could use some human kindness. I'll make something easy. Comfort food."

"Good idea."

When I got home, Pete was putting the finishing touches on a pan of veggie lasagna. "This is for tomorrow. I thought I'd put it together today, and then I can just bake it when I get home. I'll get a baguette or something, too."

"Sounds great. What are we having tonight?"

We had beef stew and salad. After dinner we both had work to do – Pete was working on his article on student psychopathology, and I was writing my article about librarians and law enforcement. We worked until about ten then went to bed. It wasn't until then that I realized that I'd forgotten to tell Pete what Clinton had said.

"Hey, I forgot to tell you. Clinton got the final word about Terry Moynihan." I told him what Clinton had said.

"That's not very helpful."

"No, but it's the best he can do. Everyone that knew Moynihan directly is dead or gone."

"Hm."

"But it does occur to me – he might be in jail."

"God, you're right. Boy, it was dumb of me not to think of that."

"No it wasn't. I didn't think of it until just now. But if he tried to live on his own, without the church's protection – what's the chance that he stopped being a pedophile?"

"Slim to none."

"Exactly. Hell, he might even be dead."

"Yeah... Kevin could find out."

"Arrest records are public record, right? Looks like Google would have caught that when I searched for him. And there were no obituaries."

"Maybe. It would still be worth asking Kevin about."

"He and I are having lunch tomorrow. I'll talk to him about it then."

"Okay, thanks. So here's your question for tonight. Did you always want to be a history teacher, growing up?"

"No. That didn't happen until my sophomore year of high school. I had a great world history teacher that year. Mrs. Lynde. She's the one who got me interested in ancient history. She really made the Roman Empire come alive for me."

"What did you want to do before that?"

"Various things – when I was really small, I wanted to be a firefighter because I wanted to ride on the fire trucks. Later in grade school I thought I wanted to be an archaeologist. I guess that was the beginning of my interest in history."

"I wanted to be an astronaut when I was really little. You never wanted to be one, huh?"

"No. The Challenger disaster happened when I was five and a half. It made quite an impression."

"Yeah, I guess it would." He rolled over to face me. "Okay. I'm ready for my question."

I watched his face closely. "If I was to find Terry Moynihan, what would you do about it?"

His pleasant expression didn't change. "I guess it depends on where he is and what he's doing. Obviously, if he's in jail, he couldn't have had interaction with Mark. Or if he's way up in the northern part of the state somewhere."

"Maybe Hunter can tell us if Mark was making jailhouse visits."

"Yeah, maybe."

"What if he's out on his own and close by?"

"Then... I don't know. But now that you've mentioned it, I'm betting he's in jail."

I hoped he was right.

Thursday, April 4

Thursday morning I texted Kevin to ask him about Terry Moynihan's record. He said he'd check. When we met for lunch, he had my answer. "Terry Moynihan has never been arrested for anything in the state of California and is not in state or federal prison anywhere in the country. We don't even have fingerprints for a guy by that name."

"Wow. How is it possible that a pedophile has never had any contact with the police?"

"That's not to say he's never had contact. But he's never been arrested. So he's never gotten caught at anything bad."

"He left the priesthood somewhere around twelve years ago, according to Clinton's timeline. What are the chances that a pedophile could stay out of trouble for twelve years?"

"Recidivism rates average about 50%. You're sure he's not living in a monastery somewhere?"

"Yeah. Clinton would have found that out."

"Hm. Listen." Kevin laid down his sandwich and turned to face me. "If you find this guy, what happens then?"

"I guess it depends on what I find. If he's not local, the chances of him having had interaction with Mark Jones are pretty slim. If he is local – then I have to decide whether to tell Pete."

Kevin picked his sandwich back up. "You're in a tough spot."

"How so?"

"If you find the guy and don't tell Pete, he'll be mad at you. If you find him and do tell, Pete's likely to do something stupid."

"Do you think he would? He's been acting pretty reasonably so far, I think."

"Yeah, but so far this is just an abstraction. If it becomes a reality, with an address and everything – I can't imagine him sitting still."

"What do you think he'd do?"

Kevin shook his head slowly. "Honestly, I'm not sure. I doubt Pete knows. It's not like an apology is going to accomplish anything at this point."

"Maybe it would."

"Do me a favor. If you do find the guy, tell me first? Then we can decide how to approach Pete with it. If he insists on going to see the guy, I could go with him."

"Good idea." Because I had to admit, I had no idea what Pete would do with the opportunity to confront Terry Moynihan.

When I got home that evening, I told Pete that Kevin had struck out. He was surprised but seemed to take it well. Hunter Mitchell was coming at 6:30, so I cleaned the guest bathroom and straightened up the living room while Pete worked in the kitchen. The lasagna smelled great and my mouth was watering when the doorbell rang.

My first impression of Hunter was that he probably got picked on a lot in school. He had the stereotypical voice and mannerisms that screamed "gay" loud and clear. I remembered that he worked as a wardrobe assistant and figured that was probably a pretty safe place for him. He was about 5'8", with bleached blond hair, wearing tight black pants and a black and white striped t-shirt.

I invited him in and offered him a drink; he asked for white wine. I went to the kitchen and poured while Pete came downstairs and introduced himself.

Hunter balanced himself on the edge of the loveseat. He seemed a little intimidated. We both towered over him – I might have felt intimidated myself in the same situation.

Pete said, "Dinner will be ready in a few minutes." I figured I'd let him do the talking, since he was the one that had known Mark.

"Thank you. It smells wonderful."

"How are you doing?"

"Oh…" Hunter studied his wine glass. "It's still really rough. I have to go on Saturday and clean out the apartment. Mark's mom is coming with me, but I am soooo dreading it." He shuddered.

"It would be tough to go back there." Pete's voice was soothing. He was using his psychologist skills.

"I couldn't do it myself. And I still don't know if I'm ready - but we have to get the place cleaned out. I can't afford the rent. I have to break the lease, but the manager said she'd waive the fee because - because of what happened."

"That's nice."

"Yeah." Hunter looked lost.

"Where are you going to live?"

"I guess I'll stay with my brother, for now, while I find a place. There's a girl at work who needs a roommate. I might move in with her."

"How long had you and Mark been together?"

"A couple of years, almost. We'd lived together for a little over a year."

I tried to think of a polite way to ask this, and couldn't. "Did Mark leave you - anything to help you start over?"

Hunter shook his head sadly. "He'd talked about changing his will, but he never did. He left everything to his mom, what there was."

"He didn't have much?"

"No. I mean he made good money, but he wasn't a saver. He spent everything he made."

The oven timer went off. Pete said, "Let me get everything on the table." He went upstairs. Hunter asked me, "How long have you two been together?"

"About nine months. But we were friends for six years before that."

"Oh, that's nice. To be friends first."

"Where did you meet Mark?"

"At a club. I was there with some friends and he was by himself - he was wearing a nice suit and he looked out of place. He told me later that it was his first night out after he broke up with his last boyfriend. So I guess he didn't know the club scene. But we started talking, and I thought he was a nice guy, and one thing led to another." He had a little smile on his face. Good memories, I hoped.

Pete came to the head of the stairs and called us to dinner. He'd set the lasagna and bread on the counter so we could serve ourselves. Hunter took a generous portion. "I haven't felt like eating much, and my brother's a lousy cook. But this smells awesome."

Pete said, "You can have some to take home if you want."

"Oh, that would be great."

We made small talk for a few minutes as we ate. Then Hunter said, "Mark's mom said you're a psychologist."

"That's right. I teach rather than practice, but I have the license and everything."

Hunter laid down his fork. "Why do people kill themselves?"

Whoa. I laid down my fork, too. Pete said, "There are all kinds of reasons. But usually, what it comes down to is that they either believe life is so bad that they can't go on, or that everyone would be better off without them. They think that because they're depressed."

Hunter's voice wavered a little. I really hoped he didn't cry. "How could I not know that Mark was depressed?"

"There are people who still function when they're depressed. It's not always like the TV commercials show it."

I asked, as gently as possible, "Had anything unusual happened?"

"No. At least, not that I know of. He'd made a couple of comments about money, though. I think he was having money problems."

"But you said he made good money."

"He did. But he was always worrying about it. He spent a lot of time checking his accounts online."

"You didn't have joint accounts?"

"No. I paid for half the utilities and a little toward the rent and groceries, but that's all I could do."

"Was Mark ever late with the rent, or anything like that?"

"Not the rent, no – but we did get a second notice on the power bill a couple of times. The first time Mark just said he forgot. The second time he asked me to loan him fifty dollars so he could pay the bill."

"He paid you back, didn't he?"

"Yeah." But Hunter looked troubled.

I asked, "Did he have a retirement account or anything?"

"He had a 401K through work. But he also had a broker that he talked to every week. So I think he had a separate account, but I don't know if it was an IRA or what."

Aha. I said, "Was the broker a local guy?"

"No, he was down near San Diego. Mark went down there a couple of times."

"You didn't go with him?"

"No. He said I'd be bored. And I probably would have been."

We all agreed that we found finance boring. Hunter said, "I wish I knew more about his finances. If he was really having problems, maybe that was why – maybe he was depressed about that."

Pete said, "It's very possible."

I asked, "Do you have any of his records?"

"Yeah – my brother went to the apartment for me and brought back a couple of boxes of files. I haven't gone through any of it yet except what I needed to get the utilities out of Mark's name." He grimaced. "I had to send them a death certificate."

Pete was sympathetic. "Yeah, you have to do all that stuff at the time when you feel least like doing it."

We'd finished eating, and I stood up for seconds. Hunter's glass was empty, and I asked him if he wanted more wine. He said, "No, I'd better not, since I'm driving. But this is good. I never knew much about wine before – I was more of a margarita guy – but Mark was teaching me some."

Interesting. Jim Lengyel had said that Mark was adamant about not drinking. "Mark knew about wine?"

"He was learning himself. He was taking a course at the time I met him. We had wine with dinner every night. We tried all different kinds. I can't really tell the difference between most of them, but Mark was getting pretty good at it."

Pete said, "Sometimes if people are depressed, they drink to make those feelings go away temporarily."

"I didn't think that was what he was doing – but now that you say that, maybe he was. When he opened a bottle, we'd each have a glass and then he'd usually finish the bottle by the end of the evening." Hunter frowned into his empty glass. "I know the police said his blood alcohol level was high that night, but I never knew him to be drunk. I thought he could hold it pretty well."

Pete and I gave each other a look. I figured that Mark was probably good at hiding things. Pete changed the subject, and we talked about Hunter's work for a while. He had some entertainingly gossipy stories about several actors that got us all laughing. After we'd eaten ice cream, Hunter said, "Thank you for inviting me to dinner. It's nice to talk about Mark to someone outside the family."

Pete said, "It's nice to talk to you about him. I never knew him as an adult."

"Mark's mom said you were talking to people. Trying to figure out what happened."

"That's mostly Jamie." Pete smiled at me. "But we haven't gotten very far."

I said, "If I had the name of the broker, I might be able to find out something about Mark's finances. He or she might not tell me anything, but at least I'd have a name. Then maybe Mark's mom or sister could look into it."

"I'll go through that box this evening. I can call you if I find anything."

"That'll work." Hunter and I exchanged phone numbers. Pete packaged up two chunks of lasagna for Hunter, and he thanked us again and left.

As we were cleaning up the kitchen I said, "It's sounding more and more to me like Mark was having money issues. And he'd started drinking after he broke up with Jim."

"Yeah, sounds like it."

I studied Pete's profile. "But you still think it had something to do with the priest."

Pete gave me a look. "You don't?"

"I'm not saying that Mark's history wasn't part of his psyche. I'm sure it was. He may have been depressed for a long time, with the abuse always there in the background. But what changed recently was his financial status. If we're looking for triggers, money seems more likely."

"You're probably right."

But I couldn't tell whether he believed that.

When we went to bed, Pete said, "Ready for questions? You go first."

"Okay. Do you ever wonder if we're not gay enough?"

"*What??*" He was laughing. "I don't know about you, but I've never wanted to have sex with a woman in my life. How much more gay can you get?"

"You know what I mean. And no, I've never wanted to have sex with a woman either. But think about all the gay guys we know. We're the butchest of the bunch."

"Nah – who are you talking about?"

I started listing men on my fingers. "First, Neil and Mark." Neil Anderson was Mel's law partner and a Marine buddy of my dad's. His husband was one of the paralegals in the office. Neither of them was swishy – Neil had been a Marine, after all – but they were into food, wine, art, and film. "Then there's the assistant chair of your department, Elliott, and his boyfriend Matt." We'd been to dinner at Elliott and Matt's place back in November. The house had been full of perfectly groomed men talking about food, wine, art, and film. "There's Aaron and Paul." A friend of Pete's from work, and his partner. Paul, the partner, was an interior decorator. We'd had dinner with them a few times and they both loved to gossip. "This kid this evening. And most of my exes."

"I thought you only dated manly men."

I laughed. "None of them would have fooled you."

"Even Ethan? It's hard for me to imagine you being with a femme-leaning guy for any length of time."

"Ethan was probably the least effeminate. His thing was working on his body. Not like a body builder, but he was obsessive about staying in shape, keeping a six-pack. And he spent a lot of time on his hair."

Pete laughed. He'd let his hair grow somewhat longer from the close-cut do that he wore during his police days, but it was still pretty short by anyone's standards. "No worries about that with me."

"Nope, you're not a bathroom hog at all."

"Are you concerned that we're not gay enough?"

"I wouldn't say concerned – but think about it. We don't like wine tastings, we don't have any connection to the entertainment industry, we're not interested in fashion or design, we don't like cruises, we don't dance, we're not into three-ways or bears or leather, and we're not raising kids or looking to do that. We like sports and we eat pizza and drink beer. We're poor examples of the gay lifestyle."

Pete laughed again. "We're not doing our part for the cause."
"Exactly."

"What do you propose to do about it?"

"I don't know. Probably nothing. But I'll let you know."

"I await your decision."

I gave him a playful smack. "Okay, your turn."

"If you find Moynihan, what's Kevin planning to do about it? Because I know you and he have talked about it."

Oy. "He wants me to tell him, too. He's concerned about what you might do."

Pete was quiet for a moment. "You're concerned too."

"Yeah, I am. So far you've accepted our lack of progress pretty calmly. And we're kind of at a dead end – I don't think we're going to find him at this point. I don't know where else to look. But if I do come across something, it worries me that you might confront him. I don't see that ending well."

"Come on. I'm not stupid. I'm not going to do anything problematic. I just want …" His voice trailed off. "I don't know what I want."

"Maybe you'd better decide."

"Yeah."

End of discussion.

Friday, April 5

I had a committee meeting first thing in the morning, then a history department meeting mid-morning. I didn't get to turn on my phone until lunchtime. When I saw that Hunter had called, I called him right back. I was afraid we'd play phone tag all day, but he answered. "Hi, Jamie."

"Hey, Hunter. Did you find anything?"

"Yeah. I found some papers from the broker in San Diego. He's actually in La Jolla. Neither my brother nor I can make any sense out of the numbers, but I do have the guy's name and phone number."

La Jolla. It had to be the same guy that Jim Lengyel had mentioned. I grabbed a pen. "Okay, go ahead."

"The name is Rob Harrison." He read off the number.

I froze. *No fucking way.* "Could you give me that again?"

He did. I managed to write the number this time. Hunter asked, "Are you gonna call the guy?"

"Yes, I am."

"Will you let me know what you find out?"

"Of course. I'll get back in touch as soon as I know anything."

He thanked me and hung up. I'd been standing at my desk, and now I dropped into my chair.

Rob Harrison.

Robbie Harrison? My childhood friend? My first sexual encounter? Surely not. It was a pretty common name.

I called Mel. I didn't expect that she'd be available, but this was my lucky day for phone connections. "Hey, Jamie, what's up?"

"Do you know anything about what happened to Robbie Harrison?"

"Robbie? Why?"

"The name Rob Harrison came up in a discussion with a guy I met. I wondered if it was him."

"Um – I know he got kicked out of Annapolis."

"Yeah, I heard that."

"I'm trying to remember who told me this. I think it was Lindy Cameron…"

Lindy was one of our high school classmates. She still lived in Oceanside and kept tabs on everyone. "What did she say?"

"She heard that Robbie's father cut him off when he got tossed from the Academy. Robbie came back to California and went to school someplace central – Fresno State, I think. Then he came back to San Diego and went to work in a bank. And he got married."

"To a woman?"

"Yeah. What's this about?"

I told Mel briefly about Mark's suicide and Pete's desire to find out what happened. "And now it turns out that Mark's financial advisor's name is Rob Harrison. In La Jolla."

"You're gonna call him?"

"Yeah."

"Well, if it's him, tell him I said hello."

"Yeah, sure. Thanks, Mel." *Shit*. The odds were better now that this Rob Harrison was my Robbie Harrison. "My" being a relative term. I looked at the clock; it was 12:15. No time like the present. I dialed the number.

A voice that I never thought I'd hear again said, "Rob Harrison."

"Robbie? It's Jamie Brodie."

Silence for a minute. Then, "*Jamie?* Oh my God. Where are you? I heard you moved to England."

"That was for my doctorate. I'm in LA now."

"Holy crap. I'm – *damn*. We should get together."

"Yeah. Actually, that's why I'm calling. I wondered if I could come down and see you." There was more tension in my voice than I'd intended.

"Um – sure, but why?"

Shit. Now he was suspicious. "It's a long story." I wasn't going to tell him anything yet. I wanted to see his face when I asked him about Mark. "Do you work on the weekends?"

"When I need to. My daughter's got a soccer game tomorrow morning, but I could meet you at the office in the afternoon. Around 1:00?"

"That's perfect. Where's your office?"

He gave me the address and brief directions. "It's great to hear from you, Jamie, but it's a little strange."

"I know. I'll explain it all when I see you."

"Okay. I'm looking forward to it."

We said goodbye. I sat and looked at my phone for a long minute. Then I called my dad to tell him I'd be stopping by in the morning.

When I got home that evening, Pete was grilling on the first-floor deck. I got a beer from the fridge and brought him up to date. "Do you want to go with me tomorrow? You could hang out with my dad while I was in La Jolla."

"Let me get this straight. You want me to come with you while you visit your old boyfriend?"

"What? He wasn't my boyfriend. We just fooled around together because we didn't have anyone else." I frowned at him. "Is this jealousy I hear again?"

"Of course not. Why would I be jealous? It was fifteen years ago, right?"

"Right. You have no reason to be jealous. But it kind of sounds like you are."

Pete sighed. "I'm not jealous. I'm just not entirely comfortable with this visit."

"There's no reason to be uncomfortable. I'm just going to ask Robbie to tell me about his dealings with Mark. It won't take long. And we could visit with my dad."

"As much as I would like to see your dad – no. I'd rather not come with you. Plus I can get a lot of work done. I had a paper due today in two of my classes so I have a ton of grading to do."

"Okay. But you can change your mind."

"Maybe." But I knew he wouldn't.

One of these days we were going to have to wrestle this jealousy thing to the floor and pin it until it gave up. But today was not that day.

When we went to bed, Pete asked the first question. "Tell me why I shouldn't be jealous of Robbie."

Hm. Was this a good or bad sign? I didn't know. "He is not someone I would ever be with in terms of a relationship. He got kicked out of the Naval Academy for drinking. He's apparently in the closet, married with kids, so he's probably living a lie. He was another spoiled rich kid – his dad was a colonel and Robbie was an only child. One of the reasons I spent so much time at his house was because their house was big and Robbie had it almost to himself. His dad was never home and his mom was always asleep. I think she took pills. Anyway, our house was crowded all the time, and going over to Robbie's gave me some breathing space. And he was completely under his father's thumb. He was afraid of his father, but he would never have confronted him."

"Sounds like another spoiled, rich boy coward. You went from one spoiled coward to another. Robbie to Ethan."

I had never considered that before. "Holy shit. You're right. I never realized that."

Pete chuckled. "We'll analyze that at another time. Any other spoiled rich boys in your portfolio?"

"Only Scott. And he wasn't spoiled, his parents were hard on him. But he was rich." I poked Pete in the ribs. "Okay. So you've got plenty of reason to not be jealous of Robbie, right?"

"Right."

"Okay. Here's my question – I forgot to ask you this last night with Hunter being here. How did it go in therapy yesterday?"

"Oh." Pete rolled from his side to his back and looked at the ceiling. "It went okay. Not very productive. She wanted to go back and rehash my teenage years. We've been over that so many times, I don't see the point."

"So what is the point? Do you think it's time for a new therapist?"

"I don't know." He gave me a look. "Are you trying to get me into couples therapy?"

"Not necessarily, although I still think that's something we need. I just wonder – I mean, I've had a couple of issues with your therapist, and it doesn't seem like you're making a whole lot of progress – maybe it's time to switch to a new kind of therapist. Maybe psychotherapy isn't the best thing for you now."

"She did have the idea about asking questions."

"Yeah, but the week before that she said I'd been coddled. And now she wants to talk about what happened twenty years ago. I just think it's something to consider."

"Yeah. I'm considering it."

"Are you?"

"Yeah."

"I think you'd like Dr. Bibbins. Not even for couples therapy, just if you went on your own."

"*Okay.* I said I'll think about it."

"Okay. Sorry. I'm not trying to pressure you."

"So stop talking. I need you to do something else with your mouth for a while."

Saturday, April 6

I left home at 8:30. Traffic wasn't bad on the 405 or the 5, and I got to my dad's about 10:30. He was working in the garden, so I joined him in the back yard. I hadn't told him why I was coming down, just that I had an appointment in La Jolla at 1:00. We talked about my nephews for a bit, then Dad asked, "What's this appointment you have?"

"I'm going to see Robbie Harrison."

My dad sat back on his heels, trowel frozen in mid-air, staring at me. "You're *shitting* me."

"No. He's a financial advisor in La Jolla, and he was the broker for Pete's friend who committed suicide. So I'm going to see what Robbie can tell me about that."

"Do you think that's a good idea?"

"Why wouldn't it be? It's not like Robbie's dangerous. I doubt he's doing anything illegal, although it's probably unethical – I just want to find out if Mark had a major financial loss that might have triggered his suicide. Mark's boyfriend didn't know anything about his finances."

"Do you think Robbie will tell you anything?"

"I have no idea. I don't know why he wouldn't. It's not like there's anything that anyone can do about it now."

I could tell my dad still had reservations about what I was doing. But he dropped the subject. He hadn't thought much of Robbie when we were kids. Robbie had always taken the path of least resistance, regardless of the situation, and my dad saw that as a character flaw. I tended to agree.

We ate lunch – Dad made shrimp and grits for me – then said goodbye. I'd go straight home from Robbie's office rather than stop in Oceanside again. I drove down to La Jolla, following directions from Robbie and Mapquest, and got to his office about five minutes early.

Robbie's office was in an upscale strip mall – what did you call it, when it was too nice to call a strip mall? – between an insurance agent and a dentist. The tasteful lettering on the door said "Harrison Investments." It seemed Robbie was operating on his own, rather than with one of the big companies. I pulled the door open and walked in.

The place was starkly decorated. There was a space for a receptionist, but no desk, just a small table with a couple of chairs. Beyond that was a hallway with three doors. As I let the outer door close behind me, Robbie walked out of his office.

He looked older. His blond hair was thinning and he'd lost his athletic physique. He had a little paunch and his shoulders weren't as wide as they used to be. If I didn't know his age, I'd put him at around forty. He smiled and held out his hand, and we shook. I was glad to not have to hug him. "Jamie! Look at you, you look great! How are you?"

"Fine. How about you?"

"Oh, fine, you know..." He trailed off. I didn't know, but I wasn't going to ask. "You got taller."

"Yeah, I think I grew another inch while I was in college."

"How's your dad? And Kevin and Jeff?"

"Dad's fine, still in the same house. He retired ten years ago. Jeff's a veterinarian in Oceanside, out east of town. He's married and got two kids. And Kevin's a cop. A homicide detective in LA."

Robbie grew a little pale. "Really. A homicide detective."

"Mm hm. Oh, Ali and Mel said to tell you hello."

"Oh my God. Are they still a couple?"

"Yes. They're in LA too. So what about you? What happened to your parents?"

Robbie rolled his eyes. "Come in to the office, sit down." He led me into his office, which was also sparsely furnished. A computer on the desk, a file cabinet to the side, in light-colored wood and steel. There were two Eames-style chairs in front of the desk, and we sat in those. "My mother died five years ago of an overdose of sleeping pills. It was ruled accidental, but I think she did it on purpose."

"Oh wow. I'm sorry."

Robbie shrugged. "You know I wasn't that close to her. It's not like she was ever a force in my life. And my dad hasn't spoken to me since I got kicked out of Annapolis. He's still at the Pentagon."

"I'd heard about Annapolis."

"Yeah. I did that on purpose. I couldn't stand it there, but I couldn't just quit. I had to make it so they wouldn't take me back."

Jeez. Robbie was still as spineless as ever. I flashed back to a memory from high school when Robbie had made a show of signing a purity pledge with his girlfriend – although he was having plenty of sex with me. When I laughed at him, he'd said, "I had to make it so she wouldn't ask me for sex." Classic Robbie.

"So you've ended up in the financial industry."

"I was at a bank for several years then struck out on my own."

"And you have a family."

"Yeah – I married Ashley when I graduated from Fresno State, and we have two girls. Elizabeth is seven and Emily is five. What about you?"

"Family? No. I live with my boyfriend in Santa Monica. He's a college professor."

Robbie's expression grew guarded. I knew that look – here came a dose of denial. "So you did turn out to be gay."

"Robbie, I didn't turn out to be gay, I was always gay. And I always told you that."

"And you said I was too."

"So you're bi, not gay." I gave him a look and he started to squirm.

"Let's change the subject."

"Okay, let me tell you why I'm here. Does the name Mark Jones mean anything to you?"

"Oh." Robbie's expression cleared. "Yes. My client that committed suicide. I was so sorry to hear about that."

"Yeah. Mark was a childhood friend of Pete's – my boyfriend. Pete and Mark's family all want to know why Mark felt he had to kill himself. We've been putting the pieces together, and yesterday, your name came up."

Robbie looked puzzled. "In what context?"

Did he really not know? "In the context that Mark had lost a whole lot of money in his investments. The investments that he had with you."

"Oh. I see. Here's the thing with Mark – he chose his own investments. I was just the broker in his case. He told me what he wanted to buy or sell and I made the transactions. I did very little advising in his case."

"Maybe you should have."

"It wasn't really my place. Mark was an actuary, he was in the business. He knew what he was doing."

"Apparently not, since he lost so much money."

"He was willing to take the risk. With his training, he understood the risks better than anyone."

"From the standpoint of professional ethics, at some point don't you have to say to a client, 'Look, this is not in your best interests?' You can certainly refuse to make a trade."

"I can, but – did you know Mark?"

"No."

"Then you don't know how insistent he was. He was determined to make the trades he made. If I hadn't done it, he would have just gone somewhere else, and I'd be out a commission. I have two children in private schools and a wife who likes nice things. I don't give up commissions." He rolled his eyes again. "It's business, Jamie. Mark knew the game and he understood the consequences. Mark's death is a terrible loss and I feel very badly for his family. But I don't see how you can pin it on me."

"No one's trying to pin his death on you. We're just looking for the trigger. When was the last time you talked to Mark?"

To his credit, Robbie looked chagrined. "It was the day before he died."

"*Really*. You don't say."

"I didn't actually talk to him, I exchanged emails with him. I'd gotten his latest statement and sent it to him."

"He didn't get his own statements?"

"No. Because he was in hedge funds. Those can't be managed through a personal account. So the statements would come to me and I'd forward them on to him."

"What did the statement say?"

"He'd sustained some losses over the prior month."

"What kind of losses?"

Robbie sighed. "Somewhere in the neighborhood of two hundred thousand."

"Holy *shit!* That's a pretty bad neighborhood."

Robbie's tone was patient, as if he was explaining something to a very slow student. "That's the nature of risk. That's what Mark understood. The markets are like Vegas. You don't play with money you can't afford to lose. Mark could afford it."

"No, he couldn't. He was borrowing money from his boyfriend to pay the bills."

"How was I supposed to know that? If a client doesn't choose to be honest with me about his financial situation, what can I do? I never had *any* indication from Mark that he was having financial problems."

This was getting me nowhere. But at least I'd uncovered the likely trigger. Mark's family and Pete would get an answer. "Where did you even meet Mark?"

Robbie turned pink again. "Uh – in LA."

Hm. "Like at a conference or something?"

"Um – more like an after-hours gathering."

Oh, really. "You met him at a bar."

Robbie shrugged. "It was a wine bar. A nice place. It was crowded, and we were both there alone, and we shared a table. We got to talking, and one thing led to another."

One thing led to another. The same phrase Hunter had used about the night he met Mark. "Did you sleep with him?"

Robbie tried to look offended, but he couldn't pull it off with me. I glared at him and he sagged a little. "Yeah."

I shook my head. "Like I said, Robbie. Gay or bi."

"It was just that one time." But Robbie had a sly look on his face that I recognized.

"Just that one time with Mark, you mean."

He rolled his eyes again. For someone who claimed not to be gay, he did a lot of eye-rolling. "Yeah, yeah."

Well. Robbie's current sex life was none of my business. I glanced at my watch; it was nearing 2:00. "I should get going."

Robbie practically leapt to his feet. "I'm glad to see you, but I'm sorry it's under these circumstances. And I am very sorry about Mark's death. If I'd had any idea about the true state of his finances, I'd have said something to him."

I wasn't sure if I believed that, but I didn't argue. We shook hands again and Robbie saw me out. Once I was in the parking lot, I took a deep breath. I felt slimy. I couldn't believe I'd ever had sex with the guy.

When I got in the car, I realized that my phone hadn't buzzed all day. That was odd. If Pete was home he would usually have been texting me on and off. I'd texted him when I'd gotten to my dad's; now I sent another one. *Leaving La Jolla now, coming straight home.*

He didn't reply. Maybe he'd turned his phone off to concentrate on work.

I got slowed up for about ten minutes behind an accident on the road around Del Mar. I was just passing the exit for my dad's house when my phone buzzed. I picked it up – and nearly drove off the road when I saw what Pete said.

Found Moynihan. Organic farmer in Winchester. Heading down there. Please understand.

Shit! Shit, shit, shit! I immediately called; it went straight to voice mail. I pulled over to the shoulder and called again. Straight to voice mail. I texted – *What are you doing!! Don't!!* – and called Kevin.

Kevin didn't answer either. Where the hell was he? At least his phone was on. Maybe he was just busy. I waited a minute – probably closer to thirty seconds – and tried again. This time he answered. "Hey."

"Thank God! Are you at home?"

"No. We're at Abby's sister's house. Abs is building us a wardrobe. What's wrong?"

"You're at Andie's? In Palmdale?"

Kevin sounded worried. "Yeah. Jamie, what's wrong? Is it Dad?"

"No, it's Pete. He found out that Terry Moynihan lives in Winchester. He's on his way there. We have to stop him."

"*Shit.* How'd he find out?"

"I don't know! I might be able to beat him there, but he didn't give me an address."

"When did he leave?"

"I don't *know*. I just got the text, so I hope just a few minutes ago. I called him and his phone is off. I need his address, Kevin!"

"Well, fuck, Jamie, how am I supposed to know that?"

"I don't know! Can't you do some cop thing?"

"Shit. I'm not supposed to."

"I don't know what he's gonna do, Kev."

"I don't think he'll do anything stupid."

"I don't *know*."

"Okay, listen. Where are you?"

"I'm on the shoulder of the 5 just past Mission Avenue."

"Okay. I'm gonna call Max, see if he can find the address and send it to you."

"Okay." I gulped. "Thanks, Kev."

"No worries." Kevin clicked off. I opened a map on my phone. Winchester was in Riverside County, off the 15. Well off the 15. *Shit.* But I was headed in the right direction. I took the next exit, for the Mission Expressway, and headed east.

I was in Bonsall when my phone buzzed with a text from Max O'Brien, another West LA homicide detective. I pulled over. Max had helpfully sent a map; Moynihan's place was on the north side of Winchester. *Damn.* Pete would be coming down the 215, which meant he'd be approaching from the north. But I had time on my side – I hoped. I got back on the road and stepped on the gas.

I finally got to the 15 and was able to speed up some. I crossed into Riverside County and passed Temecula, and started watching for Rt. 79. It wasn't too much farther. Rt. 79 was a two-lane road, but it was fairly straight. I got slowed down through town but finally got past it and back into open country – and that's where I found Moynihan's farm. I pulled into the driveway and parked – just behind Pete's Jeep. Pete was just getting out.

I jumped out of the VW as Pete turned. Pete's face was a mask. "What the fuck are you doing here?"

"I came to stop you from doing something stupid! What the fuck is the *matter* with you?"

Pete scowled. "Unfinished business. You got here awfully quick."

"I hadn't gotten into Pendleton yet. I was right where I needed to be." I tugged on his arm. "Come on. Let's get out of here before we get arrested for trespassing."

Pete opened his mouth to say something else just as a man walked around the back of the house and toward them. "Can I help you with something?"

I studied the guy. This couldn't be Pete's priest; he was too young. He was probably in his late twenties, about 5'10", brown hair and eyes. His expression was friendly but cautious. Pete said, "I'm looking for Terry Moynihan."

"Oh, Terry's not here. He had to take one of our cats to the vet. Can I help you? I'm Terry's husband."

Whoa. I was watching Pete; his face didn't change, but I could feel the ripple of shock roll through him. It didn't look like Pete was going to say anything. I said, "Ah, congratulations. How long have you been married?"

"Five years." The guy was looking back and forth between Pete and me. "What's this about?"

Pete seemed to be struck mute. I said, "My name's Jamie Brodie, and this is my friend Pete. Pete knew Terry when he was younger, and wanted to look him up."

The guy's face changed. *He knew.* "I think you'd better come up on the porch. We can talk there." He led the way and pointed to a couple of porch rockers. "Can I get you a drink? Iced tea?"

"Sure, that would be great."

The guy disappeared into the house. Pete found his voice. "What the fuck are you *doing?*"

"You came here for closure, right? I'm getting it for you."

"I didn't…" But Pete didn't get to finish his sentence; the guy was back with a tray, pitcher and glasses. He poured the tea and sat on the porch swing, facing us. "My name is Casey Mathis. I grew up on a farm in Bishop, and that's where I met Terry. He was our parish priest at the time."

Pete seemed to be struck dumb again. I asked, "How old were you?"

"Sixteen." Casey crossed his arms over his chest. "I know what you're thinking, but I knew what I was doing. We kept it quiet until I was eighteen, then Terry left the priesthood and we moved down here. Fresh start. No one knew us, no one knew anything about Terry. No one around here even knows that he was ever a priest. We've been together ever since. *Happily* together."

"So Terry told you about his – past."

"Yes. He told me everything. I made him go to counseling. We still go every week."

"That's good. I'm glad to hear that." I set my glass on the table next to him. "You know for a fact that he…"

I didn't have to finish. "Yes. I know where he is all the time. I'm with him 98% of the time. The only time I'm not is when he goes someplace specific, like today. I would have gone with him, but I needed to work on the irrigation system."

"That must wear on you, keeping tabs on him like that."

"Not really. We live and work here, we run errands together. We don't go to church. We're out here in the middle of nowhere with no close neighbors."

"What do you grow?"

Casey relaxed a little. "Kiwifruit is our big crop. But we also grow all our own vegetables, and we have some apple trees too."

"Good for you."

Casey shrugged. "I love farming. I couldn't take over my parents' farm because they kicked me out when I told them I was with Terry, so we bought this land and started our own farm."

"Taking on a relationship with a guy like Terry – that couldn't have been easy."

Casey looked me straight in the eye. "It's worth it. I love him. I told him I'd help him, and I have. I also told him that if he ever messed up again, I'd leave him. He doesn't want that. He knows he can't – on his own, he'd end up in jail."

"Does the name Mark Jones mean anything to you?"

Casey looked puzzled. "No. Should it?"

I glanced at Pete, who hadn't moved. His face still showed nothing. I said, "Mark was in Terry's parish in Barstow. He was about sixteen too. He committed suicide a couple of weeks ago. We're trying to get some answers for his family."

"Oh, no." Casey shook his head sadly. "How awful. So you were thinking that he might have had some kind of recent contact with Terry?"

"We didn't know."

"Well, he didn't. We haven't been out of Riverside County for – three or four years, at least. And no one has come here, at least not until today. And I know he hasn't had contact with him online, because Terry and I use the same computer and email address. I'd know." Casey's eyes narrowed a bit. "How did you find us, anyway?"

I looked at Pete. "I'd like to know that myself."

Pete said, "Matt Garvey."

Casey looked puzzled again. "Who's Matt Garvey?"

"Another kid from Barstow. He was twelve. His father was the one who reported Terry. He's tracked him all these years."

When Pete had said "twelve," Casey had cringed. Now he looked worried. "This Garvey guy knows where we are?"

"He didn't know exactly where."

I said, "Then how did you know exactly where?"

"I got Jon Eckhoff to look it up for me."

I shook my head in disgust. "Great, Pete. That's just great."

Casey said, "I've been telling Terry we need a security system. Maybe he'll listen now." He leaned forward and caught Pete's eye. "How old were you?"

Pete's face was carved from stone. "Fourteen."

Casey said softly, "I'm sorry. I wish there was something I could say that would make it better."

I said, "You're doing the best thing you can. Keeping him on a short leash."

Casey sighed. He looked tired. "It's all I can do. Everyone's got their purpose, right? This is mine."

I stood. It was time to go. "We're going to let you get back to your irrigation. We appreciate your candor. And I'm not going to tell anyone where you are."

"I have your word on that?"

"Yes." I held out my hand, and we shook.

"Thank you." Casey turned to Pete again. "I'm sorry about your friend. I wish I could help you."

Pete just shook his head. I said, "You have. Thank you for talking to us." I pulled Pete to his feet. "Come on." I walked Pete back to the driveway and our vehicles. "Now here's what you're going to do. You're getting in this Jeep and driving home. And turn on your damn phone."

Pete scowled, but he didn't say anything. I watched him turn on his phone. We got in our cars, and I sent Kevin a quick text. *All ok. On our way home.*

Pete did what he was told.

As I drove home my panic wore off, and I realized it had been based on fear – for Pete's safety and state of mind. Now that we were getting distance, I was getting angry. He'd obviously planned this. He waited until I was going to be gone for the day, then called Garvey, then wheedled the address out of Jon. And then he'd waited – when I'd texted him that I was on my way home, he'd waited until he thought I'd be well into Pendleton on the 5 and not able to turn around easily. He'd used my reliability in letting him know where I was to plan his timing.

My brain felt like it was boiling. I started to think about leaving him. I could move back to Westwood, find a studio apartment I could afford. The relatively drama-free single life sounded pretty appealing right now.

When we got home, Pete parked in back and I parked in front. We met in the kitchen. Pete was watching me closely, but he apparently thought I was still afraid. He held his hands out in a placating gesture. "I'm okay. It's okay."

I exploded. "*It's not fucking okay!* How fucking long have you known you were gonna do this? You *planned* this whole thing. Right down to the goddamn *second*. You knew I'd let you know when I was leaving then you *waited*. You fucking waited until you thought I'd be too far into Pendleton to turn around. You used my reliability to go off and potentially *fuck up your life!* What the fucking hell is the *matter* with you!"

Pete said, "Please stop swearing at me."

I caught my breath for a minute. "Why did you bother telling me at all? That's what I can't figure out."

"It would have been worse if I hadn't told you, wouldn't it? Plus –" he was squirming a little – "I wanted you to know where I was in case – something did happen."

I shook my head. "Un-fucking-believable. How many years have I known you, now? And this is by far the *stupidest* thing you've ever done. What the fuck were you thinking?"

"You're absolutely right. It was a stupid thing to do. But – I had to know."

I threw up my hands. "If you had waited to *talk to me*, you *would* have known. Mark's suicide didn't have anything to do with Moynihan. The day of his suicide, Robbie had sent Mark paperwork detailing his losses in the fund that Robbie had recommended. It was two hundred grand."

Pete's mouth dropped open. "Holy *shit*."

"Exactly."

"What did your friend say about that? Was he sorry?"

"He was sorry Mark killed himself. He said Mark made his own trading decisions, and Mark left Robbie with the impression that he had the money to lose." I glared at Pete. "And he's not my friend."

Pete dropped into one of the chairs at the kitchen table. "That was the trigger."

I was starting to calm down. "Yeah."

He looked miserable. "So I went to Winchester for nothing."

"Not exactly for nothing. We know he's not hurting anyone else now."

"Yeah."

My phone rang – it was Kevin. In all the emotion, I'd forgotten about him. "Hey."

"Where are you?"

"We're at home. Sorry. We were having a little – discussion."

"Yeah, I bet you were. What happened?"

"Nothing. He wasn't there. We met his husband."

"His *husband?*"

"Yeah. He's about thirty. Met Moynihan when he was sixteen at his last parish. He keeps Moynihan reined in."

"So he was one of his victims."

"He doesn't see himself as a victim."

"Listen. You need to tell Pete, it's getting really hard for me to keep all this from Abby."

"Here. Talk to him yourself." I handed Pete the phone. Pete listened for a minute – I guess Kevin was expressing a few opinions of his own. Then Pete said, "I know. I'm sorry. You can tell her."

I couldn't hear Kevin's words, but his tone sounded surprised. He must have asked Pete if he wouldn't rather do that himself. Pete said, "Yeah, I guess so. I'll talk to her tomorrow."

He hung up. "I'm going to talk to Abby tomorrow."

"Good. That's good."

"I should tell your dad, too."

"That's up to you, but you know he'd be supportive."

"Yeah, I know. I know he's picked up on the tension between us. I guess it would help him to know why."

"Yeah. So, let me ask you again. What did you think you were doing, going up there? What did you hope to achieve? This wasn't all about Mark Jones."

Pete swallowed hard. "You're right, it wasn't all about Mark. I – I didn't even know until I got there. I wanted to see what had become of him. I wanted to see that he'd paid, somehow, for what he did. I wanted to see karma at work."

"That's not what you saw."

"No. I was so shocked, when that kid said the word *husband* – and that he knew everything – and – and, hell, that he's an organic *kiwi* farmer, for fuck's sake – it was just so unlike what I'd expected. So unlike anything I'd imagined."

"What had you imagined?"

Pete laughed harshly. "Seriously? A run-down trailer with the door falling off the hinges and a few teenagers hanging around. I was still thinking of him as a guy in his late twenties, when he's over fifty now. And I never imagined him with – having anyone in his life. Much less anyone permanent."

I rubbed the back of my neck. The tension there was finally starting to ease. "Are you satisfied now? That Moynihan had nothing to do with Mark's death?"

"Yeah."

"We should call Mark's mom. And Hunter."

"Yes. Tomorrow."

I went to the cabinet and got out the bottle of Glenmorangie, poured each of us a drink, and sat down at the table. I looked at Pete, sitting across from me. There were fine lines across his forehead that I'd never seen before. He looked older, and I had a sudden vision of what he would look like in twenty years. He tossed back the first drink and poured himself another. I asked, "What made you call Matt Garvey's father?"

"I was afraid you'd come back from La Jolla with nothing. Mark has been dead for three weeks, and we'd come up with exactly nothing. I had to know. And I figured if anyone knew where Moynihan was, it would be Mr. Garvey."

"What did you say to Jon when you called him for the address?"

"Just that I couldn't tell him why I needed it and that I owed him big-time."

"You certainly do."

"I know."

"Let me ask you this. What made you think it was *okay* to call Matt's father? You've had that option all this time."

If possible, Pete looked even grimmer. He took another drink. "You're not going to like this."

"I don't like any of this."

"My therapist said that she thought it would be helpful for me to confront my abuser."

"Oh. My. *God*. Today happened because of your fucking *therapist??*"

"I told you that you wouldn't like it."

I got to my feet. "Will you *please*, now, admit that it's way past time for you to get a new therapist?"

"It wasn't the best advice she's ever given me."

"No *shit*."

Pete sighed and drained his glass. He tipped the bottle of whisky and emptied it into the glass. "I'm going to tell her that I'm done."

"She'll try to talk you into staying."

"Probably. But you're right. She's not the right therapist for me anymore. It's time to move on."

At least some good had come out of this day. I sat back down. Pete looked at me bleakly. "I'm really sorry."

"I know. You can stop apologizing."

"I owe you big-time too."

"Yeah, you do."

"I promise I'll make it up to you."

"Just promise me that you'll never do anything like this again."

"I promise."

"Okay." I covered one of his hands with mine. "I was afraid you'd end up in jail for trespassing, or assault, or worse. I didn't know if you'd taken the gun. I was afraid *you* might get shot. I was imagining all kinds of terrible things."

"I know."

"And on the drive home, I was so mad at you, I was considering leaving you."

Pete blanched. "No. Please, Jamie. Please don't leave me. I am so sorry I did this, I'm-"

"Shh. I'm not leaving you. If you'd been unrepentant, though – if you'd insisted you'd done the right thing, I would have considered it."

"And you would have been justified."

We sat quietly as we finished our drinks and for a while thereafter. Finally Pete got to his feet, a little unsteadily. "I need a shower."

"So do I. Dealing with Robbie made me feel slimy."

We took showers – separately – and got ready for bed. When we lay down, I turned on my side to face Pete, but he gently pushed me onto my back. "Show me how you do this spooning thing."

"Really?"

"Yeah."

"Okay – but if you get uncomfortable with it, tell me."

"I will."

I rolled onto my left side and pulled Pete's right arm around me. "This arm goes here." I wriggled back a little and positioned his left arm under my shoulders. "This arm goes here. Now bend your knees so they're behind mine." I left a tiny bit of space between us, but Pete pulled me against him. "See? Like two spoons in a drawer. How does that feel?"

"It feels fine so far."

"That's all there is to it."

"Hm. I think maybe I can do this."

"You're doing it. How about that?"

I could feel him smiling against the back of my head. "Yeah. How about that?"

Acknowledgements

Thanks as always to the gang: Becca, Bryan, Cheryl, Chris, Dustin, Maggie, Michelle, Michael F. #1, Michael F. #2, and Trey.

And thank you to whomever it was that invented Google Maps. I couldn't do it without you.

For updates on publication, free short (and not-so-short) stories, and other random stuff, follow my blog at http://megperrybooks.wordpress.com/ and my Facebook page at www.facebook.com/jamiebrodiemysteries.

Turn the page for a preview of Researched to Death, Jamie Brodie Mystery #4.

Oxford, England
Tuesday, May 28, 2013

"Stop pacing. You're only working yourself up more."

Duncan Crowley-Smith growled into the phone. "Easy for you to say. You're not waiting for a criminal to stroll up your path."

"Don't be daft. The man's not a criminal. He's just another mad lecturer."

"He's not going to like what I have to tell him."

"He's waited this long. He can't object to a twenty-four hour delay."

Duncan heard a car door slam. "He's here. I'll ring you when he leaves." He flipped his mobile closed.

Thursday, May 30

When Detective Inspector John Frobisher and Detective Sergeant Michael Whitcombe arrived on scene, the coroner was finishing her preliminary examination. Frobisher knelt by the man's battered head. He had bruises on his jaw and knuckles. Several objects around the room were toppled, and every drawer was pulled out and emptied, every cushion sliced open and tossed aside. Whitcombe said, rather unnecessarily, "There was a fight."

"Indeed." Frobisher straightened up and frowned. "Who is this person?"

The PC referred to his notepad. "The name's Duncan Crowley-Smith, sir. He's a lecturer at Magdalen College."

"Who reported this?"

"No one, sir. The Radcliffe Science Library reported a theft of one of their books, and they suspected this man. We found him like this when we came to investigate."

The coroner said, "He's been dead at least 48 hours. Rigor is completely resolved."

Whitcombe said, "Whoever did this was looking for something. The stolen book?"

Frobisher shook his head. "And if so, did he or she find it?" He sighed. "All right. Let's get the scene of crime officers in here."

Los Angeles
Monday, June 3

"Do you know what tomorrow is?"

Oh, shit. What had I forgotten?

I turned my head on the pillow to look at my boyfriend. Pete was propped up on his elbow, looking at me and trying not to grin. He knew I didn't know what he was talking about. *Damn.*

I decided to stick with the facts. "It's Tuesday."

"True. But not what I was going for."

"Um - it's June 4th."

"You're getting warmer. What is June 4th the anniversary of?"

I thought for a second. "Tiananmen Square."

Pete looked blank. "Really?"

"Yes."

"Huh. Okay, but again, not what I was going for." He poked me gently in the chest with a finger. "What were you doing a year ago tomorrow?"

I thought harder. Then it hit me. "The fire."

On June 4th a year ago, an arsonist had torched the apartment that I shared with my brother Kevin, burning all my belongings and rendering us homeless. I'd moved in with Pete temporarily; temporary had turned into permanent a few months later.

Now Pete's wide grin broke forth. "Yep. It's our anniversary."

"Wow." It hadn't even occurred to me that we *had* an anniversary. Yet another reminder that Pete was the romantic in this relationship and I needed to up my game in that area. "Okay, so what do you want to do? We're already supposed to go to Kevin's ball game tomorrow." My brother Kevin was the starting catcher for the LAPD Centurions baseball team.

"I know. I figured we wouldn't celebrate until the weekend. I thought we could drive up the coast, see the sights, eat some good seafood. I don't know if we could find a place to spend the night or not, this time of year, but we could make a day of it."

"Sure. That sounds good." And it did. In spite of the dearth of romance in my soul, I loved spending time with Pete Ferguson. I'd been hesitant to re-start a relationship with him. We'd dated for a while five years ago, then Pete had broken up with me to go back to his old boyfriend, a guy named Luke Brenner. That relationship hadn't lasted, and we'd worked our way back to being friends. We'd just become friends with benefits before the fire. As a matter of fact... "Speaking of anniversaries, do you remember what we were doing the night before the fire?"

It took him a second, but then he remembered and the grin returned. "Oh, yeah."

I rolled up onto my side to face him and reached out. "We could celebrate that anniversary right now."